COLORFUL, DESCRIPTIVE, FASCINATINGLY PROVOCATIVE... Andrea Hurtt's *Masquerade*, is a WONDERFUL story about relationships and consequences. Just when you think you know what happens next, you realize *THAT YOU DON'T!* Not by a long shot, because that's what deception is... a mind trick that lets you think you've got it all figured out. At least until everything unravels. This is a *FANTASTIC* first novel and I can't wait to see what stories Andrea Hurtt weaves next.

Deb White- *Staff Writer for Nerds and Beyond*

From the moment I opened *Nebraska Nights*, I couldn't put it down! I immediately connected with the characters, experiencing the *EMOTIONS* and *TENSION* as I turned each page. Enraptured in their lives, I wanted more! If you love a *SPICY, RIVETING, PAGE TURNER*, you will fall in love with every encounter, leaving you wanting more; more hunting, more passion, and more *Gene, Tom, Jessica, and Alex*!

Kimberly Raff - *Executive Director at **Foster Alumni Mentors***

NEBRASKA NIGHTS

BOOK ONE

DEMONS WITHIN US

ANDREA HURTT

LINDA STECKER

PIECE OF PIE PUBLISHING

Piece Of Pie Publishing

11923 NE Sumner ST Ste 826515

Portland, OR 97220-9601"

Thank you to everyone that's been supporting me on this crazy journey. It's been a bumpy ride, with twists and turns no one could have predicted. I hope this is just the beginning of the rest of my life, writing books you love to read!

Thank you to LS for being brave enough to put our work together out there. Almost 30 years of writing together for ourselves, this was a big leap of faith. And I am so proud of you!

~ Andrea

PROLOGUE

July 1915

Rural Nebraska

"Edith, run! Hide!" Judith screamed to her oldest daughter, then ran as fast as she could. She lifted the hem of her dress to allow her legs to gain more distance. She wanted to run to the farmhouse and lock the doors and windows. But her children were there, and she couldn't put them in harm's way.

The thing behind her was fast, and she had to lead him away.

She ran past the house, screaming her warning again and bolting for the stable. Judith didn't dare look over her shoulder.

He was right behind her. His heavy breathing, the smell of death on him, followed her.

Judith needed to get to the secondary storm shelter.

Her children were smart and had been trained, if ever there was any type of danger, be it severe weather or bandits, they were to go to the storm shelter outside the back patio.

No doubt, her screams would've awakened them and the

oldest would get them to safety. Her husband had insisted there be a secondary storm shelter, large enough to get his prize stallion underground if there was severe weather.

She ran past Guinness's stall and could hear the stallion striking the wall in agitation.

At the back of the stable, a metal door on the floor led into the storm shelter. It took all her strength to lift it just enough to slip under. Judith heard his footfalls at the barn door before his rage-filled shout, as the shelter door slammed down.

In the pitch black, she felt for the bar to secure the door.

He would not get her tonight.

She sent out a prayer that she and her children were safe. In the pitch blackness, Judith stared up at the heavy metal door.

He pounded at the door, his claws scraping against the metal.

Judith backed away from the door, deeper into the darkness.

The scraping stopped.

There was silence.

She moved closer to the door.

Had he left?

Dare she look?

Judith's hand shook as she reached toward the bolt, then she heard something grating across the metal door above her.

With a sinking feeling in her stomach, it hit her.

He'd covered the door.

She didn't know what with, but the door wouldn't budge. She moved the bar and pushed with all her might. To no avail.

The door wouldn't move. Not even the slightest.

She screamed.

CHAPTER
ONE

JUNE 2024

Gene

"Another day, another job. Same old thing," Gene Priest whispered to the steering wheel of his 1965 Ford Mustang. He'd been staring at the long road ahead, until he'd heard the quiet snore to his right.

The passenger seat held his younger cousin, Tom Priest, his chin-length, dark brown hair, hiding the fact the man was asleep. The guy was six foot five inches tall, so Tom barely fit in the front seat of the vintage car. It was a discomfort they both shared. At six foot two, his knees would occasionally graze the steering wheel, if he didn't pay attention to how he was sitting. But it had been this way for a few years now, trading off driving and sleeping in the car when they were on the road. It was the only time their height was a disadvantage. Otherwise, it was good to be the bigger body in most situations.

Like what they did for a living.

If he could call it that.

They certainly didn't get paid for what they did.

Gene sighed.

This wasn't the life he'd wanted for his cousin, but it'd turned into the family business when Tom was only nineteen.

Gene had learned at a young age that the things that go bump in the night were real. His grandmother had told him stories of monsters and other evils that were hidden in the world.

He'd thought them to be just that, stories.

Until the night his aunt was killed.

Helen was the sweetest person, always there to help when needed. The youngest sibling in the Priest family, she'd been a treasure. Her two older brothers were always ready to beat up anyone who did her wrong.

That fateful night, she'd taken Gene and Tom to the movies for the evening to give their parents a night alone. Both boys had sat in the back seat. His young cousin was asleep in the car seat beside him.

Gene couldn't remember what movie it was. They'd never made it inside.

They'd been running late.

The parking lot was full of cars, yet not a soul outside. Helen had parked her car at the back of the lot, where the only open spots were. She'd opened the door of her little sedan and stepped out, calling back to Gene to help get Tom out of his seat belt, when the attack came.

Six-year-old Gene had seen a shadow slip up behind his aunt and wrench her neck.

Helen's body had shifted.

Gene saw the monster dressed in all black, with messy dark brown hair. His eyes locked on the blood running from his aunt's neck from the monster's bite.

The creature had turned its head and grinned at Gene, like a cat that had just eaten a canary. Blood dripping down his chin and blending into his black clothes, creating a gruesome sight.

Frozen in fear, he'd watched in horror when the lights of another car suddenly appeared, causing the creature to drop his aunt's limp body and vanish into thin air.

Gene had remained still for a few more heartbeats, before daring to move. He couldn't see if the creature was still out there, but he couldn't stay in the car with Tommy any longer.

He'd carefully removed his young cousin from his car seat, exited the opposite side of the car from where his aunt lay dead, and carried the toddler inside the movie theater, where he asked them to call 9-1-1.

His father and uncle had been so devastated that it'd started them on the path of hunting what had killed their beloved baby sister.

Gene had begun hunting with his father before he was fourteen, helping with smaller monsters. Before that, his dad let him help with the weapons, cleaning them, learning their properties and what monsters they were best used on.

His uncle kept Tom out of the life. The man didn't want that for his son.

More than twenty years later, his father dead from a hunt gone bad, and his uncle now deep in a bottle, Gene continued their work, solo.

A few years ago, Tom had confronted his father while in a drunken state, wanting to know why the man was so broken.

He'd gotten a full confession, which had sent Tom straight into Gene's path.

Like his uncle, Gene didn't want Tom to be a hunter. However, he'd be lying if he didn't admit it was nice to not be alone anymore.

They'd just finished a long and exhausting case in Colorado. It was never easy when kids were involved. An abandoned mental hospital, tucked neatly away in a suburb, the town didn't even know they had a problem.

Until seven teenagers had gone missing. Turned out they'd dared each other to stay the night in the old asylum, to face the ghosts of over six hundred and forty children and young adults who had died there sometime between 1940 when it opened, and 1992 when it'd closed.

Gene and Tom had found six of the kids in various conditions, all needing hospitalization. The seventh kid had disappeared. They'd exhausted all resources, including finding the mass burial location of the deceased residents, salt and burning the bones, and making sure the spirits had all been set free.

However, there was no sign of the missing teen. It'd been hard to walk away, feeling like their job wasn't done yet. There was nothing else they could do.

Tom made another snoring sound, bringing Gene's thoughts back to the moment.

He gave his cousin a hard shove. "Dude, can you be any louder? I can't hear myself think," Gene said.

Tom woke up with a start, making him laugh at the shocked look on his cousin's face.

"Where are we?" the younger man inquired.

"The hell if I know. We're on US-38. Gonna stop for gas soon."

When they moved on to a new location, they always avoided the main highway; back roads were the better way to go. The plates on the Mustang were real, but the date on the tags were stolen.

Gene hadn't paid taxes on the car since he'd taken possession when his dad died. Their glove box was full of fake IDs and government badges, things they needed to get into places when on a job.

If they were to be pulled over, it would be the end for them. That couldn't happen.

They had work to do.

• • •

Gene pulled the vintage car into the gas station in the small town of Broken Bow, NE, glad to find a place out in the middle of nowhere. Sometimes they took too much of a chance taking the back roads. They kept two cans of gas in the trunk, just in case. Once they'd run out of gas, and he swore to never let that happen again.

"I know you're anxious about getting back home for a while, but I think I have a job?" The younger man said, holding out a local newspaper when he returned to the car. "They've got a handful of dead people. No leads."

"*Animal Attacks Cause Citizens To Worry*" the headline read.

Gene quickly scanned the article. "It could be a case, or it could be a hungry bear."

Tom stared, "When has a bear attacked and eaten multiple people? Says here that there have been three animal attacks in the last month."

"What do you think, Werewolf? Wendigo? Ghoul?" Gene asked.

"Could be. We'd have to see the bodies to know for sure."

"Well, it's too late for that tonight. Let's get some grub and go from there. I saw a dive bar just down the road."

CHAPTER
TWO

Alex

"You want me to go in there?" Alex's voice wavered.

"You said you always wanted to live on a farm, away from everything," Jessica reminded her friend.

"I didn't think it would be this far away from everything."

"Yeah, come on. It'll be great. No boss, no traffic, no men…"

Alex didn't miss the last words, even though Jessica barely breathed them.

She stared out of the dirty windshield of Jessica's old rundown van.

Even though the sun had already set, there was still enough light to see the old three-story farmhouse before them. A door was in the center of the first floor, with large windows on either side.

The second floor had four windows across, and the third floor, presumably an attic, was split in two, with an oval window on the right side, and a standard rectangular window on the left. The wood slates of the old place needed a fresh coat of white paint; there were large chips of paint missing all over the building. To the right of the house was the large red barn.

The van rocked slightly, bringing the girls back to the moment.

"We need to get them out before they tip us," Jessica teased.

Alex groaned.

It'd been a long day in the van, especially after the air conditioner broke. Not to mention, hooked to the back of the van, was a horse trailer containing two pissed-off horses.

"Let's at least get the horses in the stable and take a few things into the house to get us through the night," Jessica said. "I don't want to unload the whole van in the dark. Besides, I think we should clean the house before we move everything in, don't you?"

Alex didn't want to get out of the van. She couldn't believe her best friend had convinced her this was a good idea, to pack up her entire life in Colorado, quit her job, and move away from everything she knew.

A fresh start? Felt like a death sentence.

She sighed when Jessica spoke.

"I'll get our bags out of the van and see if we have some hot water for showers while you let the horses out. We could go get a bite to eat at the bar we passed, right off the main highway. I don't know about you, but I could use a drink tonight."

Alex didn't answer. She just climbed out of the van. She was going to need a lot more than one drink to sleep in this creepy old house. She grabbed a flashlight out of the tack room of the trailer and headed to the barn.

It was a two-story red barn straight out of a picture book. Alex shined the light around.

The old barn looked structurally sound. It would take a couple of weeks to clean it up, but there was room for several horses there.

The stalls on the left all had attached paddocks, so she checked the first two stalls to see if the fence was secure and would hold her horses.

It satisfied her. The place was safe for the large beasts.

. . .

*Jessica

Jessica held her breath as she turned the key to the door to the old farmhouse. The ancient skeleton key felt strange in her hand, and it was a toss-up whether or not it'd work.

The attorney told her the place had water and electricity and they'd covered the furniture to keep off the dust.

She still remembered clearly when the older man had called to tell her of the new acquisition three months ago. Her Great Aunt Marge had died a spinster.

Mr. Figs, the attorney, explained the house had been passed down for four generations, always to the eldest daughter. Marge had no children of her own to pass it to, so they tracked down Jessica's mother.

Great Aunt Marge had been her mother's only aunt. Her mother, Jenifer, was an only child—as was Jessica—and she didn't want the property. She had a beautiful house in a big city and had no interest in living on a farm.

So, it went to Jessica.

The only time Jessica had been there was the summer she was twelve. It'd been her father who insisted they come to visit family since he had just lost his favorite aunt and uncle to old age.

He didn't want his wife to miss another chance to see her aunt before her time came. Jessica's mother had complained the entire three-day drive from Portland. They barely stayed forty-eight hours before they headed back home.

Jessica couldn't remember much about the house, but she remembered liking the eccentric old lady that lived there, and the peppermints she kept in a glass jar in the living room.

The musty smell of the elderly and dust permeated her nose as she pushed the door inward. All the curtains were drawn and lights were out.

Even if there'd been a hint of light outside, she still wouldn't have been able to make anything out. She touched the wall and slid her fingers carefully along until she came across the light switch.

Jessica squinted in the darkness, trying to figure it out. It wasn't an up-and-down switch like she was used to. It was a push button. She could feel two, one that was extended, was on top, and one that was almost flat.

She pushed the top button in until it clicked and pushed the bottom one out. Instantly, the room was filled with light. One lamp across the room popped and sizzled as the light bulb popped. "Shit!" Jessica gasped at the unexpected explosion, her heart racing a million miles an hour. She rested her hand on her chest, trying to control her breathing before walking to one of the large windows at the front of the house.

She unlocked it and shoved it upward with all her might. It was stiff and didn't want to open, but the house desperately needed to be aired out.

It finally budged about four inches after considerable elbow grease.

"Better than nothing," she said to the empty room before moving on to all the windows in the room, attempting to open every one of them.

Jessica wanted to uncover all the furniture and see what the place was like, but she needed to see about getting some dinner. She was getting hungry, and if her friend didn't eat soon, her blood sugar would get too low and Alex would become unbearable.

They wouldn't be able to get to a grocery store until tomorrow and she needed more to eat than cookies and Reese's Pieces.

Jessica moved through the dining room and into the kitchen, turning on the lights. The sight caused her to smile. The walls were covered with a white floral wallpaper and someone had painted all the cabinets a soft pink.

It was all very feminine. She quickly checked to see if the water was running before making her way upstairs to see about the shower situation. Jessica climbed the wooden staircase, her hand sliding along the beautiful banister. Upstairs, there were five closed doors on this level, and another flight of stairs leading to the attic.

She walked over to the first door on her right and opened it. It was a small bedroom with a twin-sized bed in it. She closed the door and moved down the hall to the next door.

It was a bigger bedroom with a turret-style window seat and a queen-sized four-poster bed. She'd always wanted a window seat to sit and read in. Jessica smiled as she opened a couple of windows in that room to get some fresh air in. She spotted the horses out in the corral but didn't see Alex.

As the second window slid up, she felt someone standing behind her. She whirled, expecting to see Alex, but there was no one there.

She'd heard the screen door slam and looked back out the first window. Alex was walking from the front of the house carrying a bucket of water.

Jessica smiled. She must've just heard Alex downstairs. She walked across the hall past the stairwell and opened the other door on the front side of the house.

It was another bedroom. Not as big as the one she was claiming, but bigger than the first. She closed the door and moved to the next room.

It was a bathroom. Jessica remembered the claw-foot tub and was so glad to see it was still here. It was larger than an average size tub, and she couldn't wait to have a good soak in it.

There was a circular rod running around the top of it, but no shower curtain. She sighed. She had a shower curtain somewhere in the van, but she didn't know where, and this one needed a curtain to go all the way around the tub and protect the wall.

Well, she'd have to make one.

She could use the smaller room to set up her online sewing business. She didn't really need a job anymore, once she'd inherited the estate. There had been investments and war bonds that had proved enough to support her and Alex for a long time.

However, Jessica loved to sew, and she had found her niche making custom quilts.

She turned the faucet on the tub. She looked around as the pipes began groaning. The sound was creepy in this old house, sending another chill through her. Her eyes darted around.

This was always the part in the scary movie where the stupid girl died.

"Don't be ridiculous! This isn't a scary movie," Jessica said aloud.

It was an old house, and the pipes hadn't been used for months. Hopefully, that was what it was. Otherwise, she'd have to call a plumber because she didn't want to live with it making that much noise.

Alex

Alex let the two large horses out of the trailer, allowing them to sniff around and munch some grass before heading into the barn. She took one horse in at a time since they weren't used to being in a barn.

Alex tied Anduril, the large red horse, to the trailer. He was a sixteen-hand chestnut gelding with a white star on his head and two white socks on his front feet.

She gave him a solid pat on his rump before grabbing Ellie's lead to get her into the barn.

Anduril would go anywhere Ellie did, so if she could convince the mare to go in, her gelding would follow.

The mare was a fifteen-hand red and white paint. She was the softest horse Alex had ever encountered, but the most stubborn mule in the world.

Alex got a reminder of then, when she almost fell backward, the lead in her hand the only thing that kept her upright.

Ellie had halted.

She glanced back to see her stopped at the edge of the door. "Come on, girlie, it's okay," Alex coaxed.

Ellie wouldn't budge. The mare planted her feet and would not cross into the barn.

Alex tried walking around outside again before heading to the barn. Each time, the horse stubbornly planted her feet at the doorway and wouldn't cross in.

She always stopped at the same place. Why?

Alex would have to see if she could convince Anduril to go in.

She repeated the exercise with him, but it had the same result.

He stopped right at the door of the barn.

Tired and frustrated, Alex checked out the round pen nearby. It was supposed to be used for training, but it would do until she could convince them to go into the barn.

The corral was overgrown with grass, and they happily began munching away while Alex went in search of water.

There was an old pump between the house and the barn. She pumped the handle to draw some water.

"Prime it."

The words whispered in her ear.

Alex paused and looked toward the house.

Had Jessica called to her, and she had barely heard it over the sound of the pump?

Jessica wasn't visible on the porch or at any of the windows.

She resumed her pumping, and she heard the voice again.

This time, it sent a chill down her spine.

Alex quickly took her bucket into the house to look for the kitchen sink.

She halted at the sink, breathing hard and trying to calm herself. She watched the water run into the bucket.

Alex was familiar with operating pumps. She hadn't *really* heard a voice. It must've been her own inner voice. Or it was just her imagination getting the better of her in the creepy old house?

She took a big breath that made her feel a lot better. She returned the bucket to the corral for her horses and then went to clean up. She'd feel even better after a meal and a good night's sleep.

On her way in, Alex picked up the two suitcases sitting on the front porch and carried them inside. She glanced around as she started up the stairs and paused halfway up. "Jessica," she called. Alex continued up the stairs. She looked around. There were lights on in the front bedroom and the door was open, as well as in the bathroom across the hall. That was strange she could have sworn she saw Jessica moving around downstairs. Of course, Jessica could have come up and left the lights on and gone back down before she'd even come into the house.

She carried her best friend's suitcase to the bedroom, assuming that was the one she chose. She left hers at the top of the stairs and went down to get their overnight bags and bring them in.

Jessica

Jessica started the water in the tub. She cringed. It was coming out a little discolored.

She let it run to see if it cleared up, hurrying to check the other room upstairs.

Alex's suitcase was sitting at the top of the landing.

That's weird. If Alex brought it up, where's mine?

It wasn't like Alex to take one and not the other. She'd left them on the porch when she came in so she could get the lights on first.

She headed back downstairs to find Alex.

Alex was pulling a few bags out of the van when Jessica found her.

"Hey, where's my suitcase?" Jessica asked.

"It's in your room."

"How did you know what room?" Jessica asked.

Alex sighed and stopped what she was doing. "Because you left the door to that room open and the light on."

"How did I not see you go in there?"

"I guess because you were in the kitchen," Alex said.

"But I haven't been in the kitchen since *before* I went upstairs."

"I saw you headed toward the kitchen when I was going up the stairs," her bestie insisted.

"Are you sure you saw somebody?" Jessica asked.

"Well, no. I just thought I caught a glimpse of you. But if it wasn't you, then where were you?"

"I was upstairs checking out the bathroom."

"Oh, maybe I just saw a curtain move or something. You do have the windows open," Alex said, sounding completely reasonable.

Jessica relaxed a little. Alex didn't do well with scary things. She didn't want to spook her, especially tonight. She should be relieved that her friend sounded so comfortable and logical. "Well, the plumbing works. I'm flushing some water through right now, then we can shower and go get something to eat."

"Great, because I'm starving," Alex said.

Jessica picked up an armful of bags and headed toward the house. "Hopefully, the water has cleared up. Showering will be messy because there's no curtain."

"I can find the shower curtain," Alex said, following her into the house.

"It's all right. I'll need to make one for it. A standard one won't fit. We'll just manage it tonight and put some fabric on the list of things to get tomorrow."

"Yeah, that ought to be fun," Alex mumbled.

"Why do you say that?" Jessica said, cocking her head to one side.

"Where was the last big town you saw?" Alex complained.

"I'm sure there's a big box store around here somewhere. I was more interested in finding the house than looking for downtown Broken Bow."

Jessica showered first, while Alex decided on a room.

"It's all yours!" Jessica said through the doorway as she went to her new room wrapped in a towel. She plugged in her hot rollers while she got dressed. Pulling her favorite shirts and dresses out of her garment bag, she gave them a good shake before she hung them in the closet. She stared at them while she put her curlers in.

"What should I wear tonight?" she asked the empty room.

"The red dress," a voice whispered, floating around her.

She looked around but didn't see anyone.

"Alex?"

Her friend didn't appear.

Had Alex spoken?

Maybe she was really tired and hungry.

Imaging things.

She looked back at the clothes. Jessica hadn't thought of wearing a dress, but it might be nice to feel a little confident tonight. She smiled as she finished rolling her hair.

Alex poked her head into the room just as she was putting the last pins in her hair.

She had let her curls hang down her back but had pulled part of it back on the side, pinning it in place with a red flower.

"You ready?" her best friend asked. Alex was wearing a black and mint dress with a black belt and black stem heels. She'd blown her black hair straight, but the ends naturally flipped outward.

"Yeah, I just need a little lipstick and I'm ready!" Jessica said. She applied the bright red lipstick, and they headed down to the van.

Maybe it was the dirt on the windshield of the vehicle or their tired eyes.

Jessica was ashamed to think about it, but the place reminded her of something right out of a scary movie. She loved scary movies, but Alex did not.

The tavern was a rundown building on a two-lane road. There

was an equally rundown gas station across the street and a few shabby homes further down the lane.

"Are you sure they serve food here?" Alex asked, her voice as skeptical as her arched eyebrow.

"No, but I sure hope they do. I don't want to drive an hour to a bigger town," Jessica replied.

The girls stepped out of the van and headed inside.

CHAPTER
THREE

*Tom

"I just don't think thaa…"

Tom glanced up from his computer when his cousin, stopped talking mid-sentence, his jaw slack, a bottle of beer midway to his mouth.

He gaped like a struggling fish for a moment before setting his beer down, without drinking a single drop. The deep green eyes of the guy, who was four years his senior, were fixed on something. Or someone…

"Well, well. What do we have here?" Gene smiled as the two women walked in.

One was a tall brunette woman in a bright red dress that hugged her slender, curvy body, followed by a shorter, also dark-haired female in a light green and black dress.

Both girls seemed way too overdressed for this little dive bar.

"I don't know, Gene. I think they may be out of your league," Tom said, glancing at his cousin.

They watched the girls walk up to the bar.

"No such thing as being out of my league," his cousin replied, smiling arrogantly. He pushed his chair back and strode over to the bar. Gene leaned one arm against the bar, and struck up a conversation.

Tom shook his head and turned back to his computer.

"Is he always this cocky?" A soft female voice asked.

The shorter brunette—the one in the black and green dress sat at the opposite side of her table so she was facing him, although her eyes were on his cousin and the one she'd come in with. Her forearms rested on the table while her fingers played with the glass in front of her.

"Always." Tom smiled. He watched her cheeks flush a little when she smiled back, then finally looked his way.

Gene still stood at the bar, talking to her friend.

They seemed to be into a decent conversation, so Tom looked back at the girl across from him.

She'd picked up her menu and was obviously trying not to notice him. She had shoulder-length black hair that seemed to have hints of blue, or maybe it was the neon lights. Her eyes were a soft, appealing brown. Her red lipstick accentuated her full lips.

She sat up straight in the hard wooden chair with her feet crossed at the ankles instead of leaning back on the chair, her skirt flowing softly around her. She seemed too proper for a place like this.

It intrigued Tom. "So, what brings you ladies to a place like this?" he asked.

She met his gaze. "Same as you I'd imagine. We were hungry."

Her eyes lit up when she smiled, and Tom wanted to see her smile again.

"You're dressed awfully nice for this place," he said.

"We dress like this most of the time," she replied.

He glanced at her friend, then back at her, taking in her light green dress. "Well, you both look great."

"Thank you." She blushed. "I'm Alex. My friend over there," she nodded toward the tall woman, "is Jessica."

"Tom. And that's Gene, flirting with your friend."

"So, what brought you and your friend here?"

Tom cast a quick look at Gene. "My cousin and I are just passing through. We just finished a job and we're looking for another."

"What kind of work do you do?"

"We… consultants."

"And you travel a lot for that?" she asked curiously.

"Yeah, we're on the road most of the time," he said truthfully.

"That must be hard. Never having time to settle and be with people you love."

"It's hard, but we manage. We've always got each other," Tom said, glancing at Gene again. "Sorry, that probably sounded cheesy."

"No. I get it. Jessica and I are family by choice. Both are only children. It's nice to have a sister I can count on."

"Gene and I are kinda the same. You'd think we were brothers that way we fight."

She nodded, polished off the small glass of liquor she was drinking, and placed it on the table.

Tom noticed a slight tremor in her hand. He watched her, to see if she showed any other signs of nerves.

Her eyes darted around the room, as if keeping an eye out for trouble.

He flagged down a server to order her another drink.

"What can I get you?" the server asked.

"*Disaronno* on the rocks. And a cheeseburger, please," she said.

"Would you like fries with that?"

"Yes, please."

"You can just put that on my tab," Tom said.

The server nodded and walked away.

"Thank you. You didn't have to do that," she said, but her voice was genuinely grateful.

"No problem. So are you just passing through or…?"

"Jessica and I are moving here."

"Here," he asked, pointing at the table. "There's not much here."

"Tell me about it!" She laughed with a sarcastic edge. "Jessica inherited a very old farmstead, about five miles from here, so we checked it out. Worst-case scenario, we fix it up and sell it, I guess." She didn't sound convinced of the idea herself. She looked up at the ceiling and let out a deep breath.

Tom could tell something was wrong. "But it's more than that," he prompted.

"It's nothing but... I just thought..."

"What?" he asked.

"I'm afraid it's haunted," she whispered. She dropped her chin in what could only be embarrassment.

Tom's left eyebrow went up. "Haunted, truly?"

She looked up at him. "It's stupid, I know."

"It's not stupid. What would make you think that?"

"What would make you think what?" the woman in the red dress—Jessica—asked, stepping up to the table.

"Oh, it's nothing." The ebony-hair girl said, blowing it off. Her eyes begged Tom not to say anything.

Tom looked up at the brunette and smiled. "That you just moved here, and the house is kinda creepy."

The woman sat down next to him. "Well, yeah. It doesn't help that we're in the middle of nowhere," she agreed. "And I think the place is over a hundred years old, or something. It's been in the family for something like four generations."

Gene joined them, next to Tom.

"I'm Jessica," the brunette said, holding out her hand for Tom to shake.

"Tom," he replied, taking her hand.

"I'm sure Tom can look up the nearest shopping places for you," Gene said, pointing to the computer.

"Oh, yeah. Sure. No problem," he agreed.

Before he could begin typing, the server returned with Alex's drink.

"Did you want to order?" Jessica asked her friend while the server was still there.

"I already did," she replied with another appealing flush of pink to her cheeks.

"Oh, well then, I'll have whatever she's having," Jessica told the server.

"That's very trusting of you," Gene said. "If I did that with Tom, I could end up eating seaweed or something."

"Alex and I have been friends for almost twenty years, so I know I'll like anything she'd order. Now she may not like the things I order..." Jessica laughed.

Tom glanced at the beauty that was Alex.

He was relieved and disappointed. He'd had a psychic tell him his soulmate was out there and would need his help. In his line of work, this was something he took seriously.

Since that day, he had been on the watch for her.

His soulmate.

However, the psychic had said her name was Jade. So, Alex couldn't be that girl. Not that he wanted to believe in that sort of thing, but after all he'd seen, he knew it could be true.

"I need to wash my hands before I pick up a burger. Who knows what I touched on the bar," Jessica said. "Alex, care to join me?"

"You know I'm not afraid of a few germs."

"Alex, you really should wash your hands," Jessica pushed.

Tom tried his best not to laugh at the obvious hint the brunette was laying out. She probably wanted to talk about Gene.

He enjoyed the view as they sauntered into the ladies' room.

"So, what do you think?" Gene asked.

"What?"

"What do you think about these two? Damn, that brunette is something. She's a spicy one. I'd like a bite of that. But you...I know you. You've got that look about you. It's rare for you to even glance a woman's way; you're always knee-deep looking for the next job. She's got something. Not sure what, but something's going on."

Tom sighed. "Alex thinks she may have a ghost. She's scared and doesn't want her friend to know."

"So it's *another* job?"

"An easy job but, yeah. It's a job," he said. "Besides, it might be beneficial to get more information about the disappearance?"

"Might be nice to have some decent company in the meantime," Gene agreed.

"As long as we don't forget why we stopped in this tiny town," Tom reminded him.

CHAPTER
FOUR

*Jessica

"Gene is actually taller than me in these heels!" Jessica said excitedly while the cold water rinsed the soap from her hands. "Oh, and those green eyes!"

Alex just laughed. "And the fact that he's hot enough to melt butter doesn't hurt."

"Well, there's that," she agreed, smiling. "Tom isn't bad either," she continued.

Alex blushed profusely. "He has a great smile," she admitted.

"And the prettiest hair!"

"Jess!"

"I'm serious. It's rare to see a guy with hair almost to his shoulders that looks well cared for. Usually, it's greasy or unbrushed. He has really nice hair," Jessica said. "This town might not be too bad after all." She could tell her friend was having major doubts about the new life they were starting.

"I hate to be the bearer of bad news, but they're just passing through. Besides, you said we moved here to get away from men and the trouble they bring."

"Yeah, true. I've never encountered a guy like Gene, he could be worth the trouble. Well, at least we have tonight. Might as well have fun." Jessica turned on her heels, ready to make the most of the night.

Tom walked back to their table a moment after they'd returned and set a glass next to Alex's plate before returning to his seat.

"Thank you," Alex said.

"You're welcome," he replied.

Jessica smiled. Tom didn't even notice she was there. He only saw Alex. She was glad. Her friend needed a guy like that right now. She looked up and smiled as Gene stood from their table.

"The server is taking too long. I'm going to the bar to get another drink. Can I get you one?" he asked Jessica.

Her glass was still half full. "I'm good thanks, I gotta drive home."

"Hmm, a lightweight, good to know," Gene teased.

Jessica just shook her head and started on her burger. When she was done, she took her own advice to enjoy the night. She needed a reminder that not all guys were psychos. She challenged Gene to a game of pool.

"Okay, but I'll warn you. I'm pretty good," he smirked.

"Then maybe you can teach me how to handle a cue stick," she teased.

Gene's eyebrows flew up as he followed her to the pool table. They each grabbed a cue stick and he racked the balls.

Jessica casually put some chalk on the end of her stick.

"Do you want to break?" he asked politely.

"Sure," she said, moving to the end of the table. She hit the balls just hard enough to make them roll a quarter of an inch. She looked up to see Gene smile.

"You need a little more power behind it," he said, lining up a shot and hitting the balls harder than she did.

"Well, are you gonna show me how or what?" she challenged.

The hot guy grinned, the joy hitting those green eyes like a shining light. He walked around behind her, leaned his cue stick against the wall, and bent over behind Jessica, lining up a shot.

Jessica held back, really wanting to press her backside against the hardness of his abs. "Not yet," she whispered to herself.

**Tom*

Tom glanced at Gene and Jessica. "He's in seventh heaven," he said.

Alex laughed out loud. "Yeah, she's got him eating out of the palm of her hand."

"Now, if she just made pie, we'd never leave."

"Pie?" Alex asked, looking at Tom, one dark eyebrow arched.

"Gene loves pie."

"What kind of pie?"

"Any kind of pie."

Alex laughed again. "Better find a place in town to stay. I think you're stuck. Jessica wins the State Fair Pie Competition every year."

Tom smiled, wishing they *could* stay. They never stayed anywhere long. Part of the job. Yet, it wasn't just the unwanted homesickness for a home he'd never had. He'd only just met this woman, but had such a draw to her. Something he'd never felt before.

"Thank you for not ratting me out." She broke his wandering thoughts.

Looking back at his computer so she wouldn't guess his thoughts were on her, he answered with, "My pleasure." Tom tapped quickly on his keyboard. "So, what makes you think the place could be haunted?"

She took a deep breath. "I don't know that it is. The place just gives me the creeps."

"Anything specific?"

"My horses refused to go in the barn, but it was pretty dark, and I've never put them in a barn before. I don't know, it's just like somebody's watching me sometimes. And I thought I saw someone downstairs when Jessica was upstairs. But it could have just been a curtain moving, so it's likely nothing."

"Let's see if we can find out." Tom reached over and pulled a chair next to him.

Alex moved into the seat, taking her drink with her.

"First, we set up a decoy," he said, bringing up an additional screen on his laptop. He googled Walmart and brought up the closest location. Then he went back to his original screen.

"Walmart?" Alex inquired.

"In case Jessica comes back over here. A quick click and she doesn't know we're researching her new home. So…being that it's an old farmstead, does the house have a name or is it under a family name maybe?" he asked.

"There was a sign over the driveway that said Ferguson Farm," Alex said.

Tom typed in Ferguson Farm, Nebraska, and hit search. He looked at a few websites that came up before he found what he was looking for. It was an old newspaper clipping.

"Girl Saved By Ghost" was the headline.

Alex leaned in to look over his shoulder.

Tom caught the scent of her perfume and was momentarily distracted. It was sweet and musky, and he wanted to move closer for another whiff. He cleared his throat and began reading quietly. *"Local girl, Marjorie Ferguson, age eight, says a ghost saved her. Her family had gone to town to sell vegetables at the market when the tornado came through last week. Marjorie says she was playing with her dolls when the ghost of her grandmother appeared to her and led her to the shelter before the storm hit. The child indicated the ghost stayed with her until the storm ended and was safe for her to leave the shelter. Although the tornado did not reach the Ferguson house, there was debris scattered around the farm. The family said they'd never seen a ghost before and that it was purely the child's imagination. Marjorie's grandmother, Judith, disappeared mysteriously after the murder of her husband, leading the sheriff to believe that she had killed him and run away, never to be heard from again."*

"So, there is a ghost," Alex said, relaxing back in her chair. She'd gone pale as a sheet and her hands were trembling in her lap.

He put a hand over both of hers. "Hey, we don't know that. We just found one story. But don't worry, we'll help get this figured out, all right?"

She nodded.

"Here, finish this. You'll feel better," Tom said, handing her the glass of *Disaronno* he'd brought her.

She slammed the rest of it.

"Do you need another?" he asked.

Alex nodded

He flagged down the server and ordered another for her and a beer for himself. He closed the window on his computer and switched back to the Walmart window. "How long have you been in the house?" he asked.

"About an hour," she said.

"An hour? And you're already thinking it's haunted?"

"Yup," she said, staring off beyond him.

"Come on, we need to distract you." Tom stood and held out a hand to her.

She looked at him skeptically for a moment, then took his hand.

He led her over to the dartboard and tried to teach her how to play.

*Gene

•   •   •

Gene racked up a second game of pool for him and Jessica. "Do you need help again with the break?" He smiled crookedly at her.

"Nah, let's see how good of a teacher you were," she winked. She hit the balls so hard she knocked two in.

"Much better," he said, crossing his arms around the pool cue.

Jessica stalked the table, looking for her next shot.

Gene's eyes were glued to her hips swaying back and forth. His eyes traveled down her long, shapely legs. They stopped momentarily to glance at the tattoo of a green vine that traveled up her right thigh, disappearing under the hem of her tight dress. She was beautiful, no doubt about that. He'd lost track of what she was doing till he heard the balls crack again. His gaze flicked to the table as another ball dropped in the pocket. Was it just a lucky shot, or if he was that good of a teacher?

She crossed the table and leaned toward him. Jessica looked up at him, giving him an excellent view of her cleavage. She hit the cue ball, and it jumped the ball in front of it and knocked her ball into the side pocket.

"Wait, a minute! I'm an excellent teacher, but that was a hell of a shot," Gene said, coming to his senses.

She laughed and came around the table to stand in front of him. She leaned in close and whispered, "You really are an excellent teacher."

He huffed at her, taking a step back, frowning. "You're just a hustler, and now you think I'm some idiot you can just take."

"Ah, come on. I was just having fun," Jessica said, still smiling. She closed the space between them, resting a hand on his chest. "Besides, I rather enjoyed having you pressed up against me," she whispered.

Gene looked into her eyes to see if she was serious. He spotted lust smoldering in her eyes. "So, should we head back to your place?" he said, clapping his hands together.

She laughed. "Keep dreaming, big boy."

He frowned again. He wasn't getting anywhere with this one. So much for a one-night stand. They were few and far between, but he still had needs sometimes, and she was *seriously* making him need. However, he was still a gentleman and it was clear when a woman meant no.

Better to let this one go. I'd probably want more than just one night, and we gotta get moving.

"Oh shit, where'd Alex go?" Jessica inquired, looking frantic.

Tom and Alex were at the dartboard.

His cousin was trying, without apparent success, to teach Jessica's friend how to throw darts.

She couldn't stop giggling when she threw one and it wouldn't even stick to the board.

"You ready to head out?" Gene asked, giving up on the evening.

"Already?" Tom asked.

Jessica stepped closer to her friend. "I think someone has had enough to drink tonight."

"Hey, I resemble that!" Alex began giggling again.

"How many did she have?" Jessica asked.

Tom thought for a moment, "Five, I think."

"Five?" Jessica asked incredulously. "She ought to sleep well tonight. You must've given yourself permission," she said to Alex.

Her dark-haired friend smiled guiltily.

"Permission for what?" Gene asked.

"Permission to get drunk," Jessica said.

"You need permission for that?" He arched an eyebrow and caught his cousin's eye.

"Well, it's just our theory," Jessica said.

"What theory is that?" Tom asked, guiding Alex out of the bar.

"If you know you have to be responsible and drive, you can usually have a drink or two and keep it together. But if you know you have a driver or you have something to celebrate or something to forget, you get drunk faster because you give yourself permission."

"Well, hell. I've been doing it wrong all these years," Gene said, smiling.

Tom shook his head as he opened the door of the van for Alex.

"You're still gonna come up to the farm and help us, right?" she asked.

"Yeah, I'll see you there tomorrow."

Standing at the driver's door with Jesica, Gene heard the fear in Alex's voice as she spoke. "I don't know why you'd want to help us. I mean, there's nothing you could do to protect me from a ghost, anyway."

Tom glanced at Gene and Jessica. "I can protect you and I will," he said seriously.

"Why would you do that?" Alex asked.

"Because you asked me to."

She leaned over and pressed her mouth to his.

Gene had to look away. Partially because it was the right thing to do, and because he was leaving without any luck.

Jessica moved past him and climbed into the van.

"Well, thanks for the evening. It was a lot of fun," she said.

"Yes, ma'am," Gene replied.

Jessica smiled and stuck the keys in the ignition. She turned the key, and the van made a groaning noise, but wouldn't start. "Come on!" she said, turning the key hard.

Again, the vehicle groaned but wouldn't start.

"Pop the hood," Gene said, walking to the front of the van.

Tom joined him.

"What is it?" he asked.

Gene fished around for a minute and told Jessica to try it again.

It groaned but still wouldn't start.

He closed the hood before he walked back over to Jessica. "Looks like you need a new alternator."

"What I need is a new car," she complained loudly from inside the van.

"Why don't you let us give you a ride to your place? We can get the part tomorrow and I'll get you back up and running. At least till you can trade this in," Gene said.

"Thank you," she replied. "I don't know how I can repay you."

"We'll think of something," he winked.

Tom retrieved Alex from the passenger side and held her hand as they walked to their Vintage Ford Mustang.

"Wow! Nice car!" Jessica said, trailing a fingertip across the smooth black paint of the car. "Complete with orange racing stripes!"

"Thank you," Gene said, pride filling his whole form. "But the stripes are gold," he corrected, while he walked around to get in.

Tom opened the other door, pushed the passenger seat forward, and helped Alex climb into the back seat.

Jessica waited to slide in next to Alex, but Tom moved into the back seat, leaving the front passenger seat for Jessica.

Gene grinned, looking forward to having someone other than his cousin sit shotgun. "Don't let her get sick back there," he said, making eye-contact with Tom in the rear-view mirror.

"I'm not that drunk, ya know," Alex said defensively.

He smirked, and started the engine, revving it before he peeled out of the parking lot and headed down the road.

Jessica gave him directions to the farm.

Glancing in the rearview mirror, Gene saw his cousin slip an arm around Alex and pulled her close to him. She laid her head on his shoulder as they drove back to the farmhouse.

CHAPTER
FIVE

As they drove under the sign to the Ferguson Farm, Tom looked down at Alex. She had fallen asleep on his shoulder as they drove to the house. He was hesitant to wake her, but they needed to get the girls inside and the situation assessed, so he and Gene could get out of there and find a place to sleep.

"Alex," Tom said, trying to wake her. "We're here."

With a little yawn, the dark-haired beauty awoke. She was peaceful. For about a half of a second. Alex's reaction to realizing they were back at the house sobered her up quickly. Her breathing quickened, and she seemed as if she was having a full-blown panic attack.

"Holy crap! You weren't kidding," Gene said, as he leaned toward the steering wheel, trying to see the outside of the house for the first time. They were far enough back that the headlights illuminated whole front of the house.

"I told you," Jessica replied, as he pulled the car up closer to the front door. "We should rent this house out to film horror movies in."

The girls had left some lights on in the house, he guessed, so it wouldn't be so creepy when they came back. However, the effect of the light pooling around the covered porch may have made it worse.

As he got out of the car he could imagine a ghostly figure moving in front of one of the upper windows, the shadow of something to come. He shook his head slightly, clearing the image.

"Everything good?" Gene inquired when he realized Tom and Alex were still in the car.

"Yeah," Tom responded. He was tempted to lean over and kiss those lips that beckoned him, the perfect way to help calm her anxiety about the house. Until Jessica leaned in the open the car door, ruining the moment.

"Alex is just nervous about the age of the house. Come on, let's go check it out," Jessica said.

The four of them made their way to the steps of the farmhouse, the eerie light filling the wrap-around porch.

Jessica unlocked the door and stood to the side to allow them to enter.

"Holy shit, you *did* just move in," Gene said, tugging at a sheet that was covering a piece of furniture in the living room.

"Yeah, like two hours ago," she retorted. "We pulled up to the house, unloaded the horses, got cleaned up, and went to get something to eat."

His cousin sauntered through the house, checking things out while everyone else followed. He walked through the dining room and into the kitchen, then out the side door and across the hall.

Tom let his cousin do his thing while he hung back in the kitchen, opening the pink cabinet doors one by one, peering into them, searching.

"What are you doing?" Alex asked, stepping up behind him.

"Looking for salt," he replied.

"Oh. Well, we haven't gone shopping yet, so there aren't any groceries here."

"I know, but salt doesn't go bad, so I thought maybe the previous owners left some behind." He continued opening cabinets.

"What do you need salt for?"

Tom pulled a can of salt down from the last cupboard he'd opened. "It helps keep ghosts away," he said.

"Wait, what? How do you know that?" Alex stammered, her body vibrating with fear.

"It's kinda my job to know," he said reluctantly. She was already freaked out and the less people knew about what he and Gene did, the better.

"What do you mean, it's your job? You said you were a consultant," she said suspiciously.

"Sort of," Tom let out a deep sigh. The sound of her voice told him that this was one time he needed to be upfront and honest. "My cousin and I are hunters."

"What does that have to do with anything?" Alex asked, confusion laced in her voice.

"Not like regular hunters. We don't hunt deer and pheasants, or the like. We hunt monsters."

"Monsters?" Her dark eyes were wide, in obvious disbelief. She ran her fingers through her hair, turned, and walked out of the kitchen the way they'd come.

"Alex, wait," Tom said, following her.

Was I wrong about telling her?

He'd never questioned his choices like this before. He reached out and caught her arm, turning her back around.

There were tears in her eyes.

"Alex, what's wrong?" He reached to wipe them away.

"I knew you were too good to be true," she cried.

"Alex," Tom paused and blew out a breath. This was the part of his life he hated. "I'm sorry I wasn't upfront with you. It's just that most people are better off not knowing about the things we go after."

"So, that's how you knew how to look it up on the Internet? I must sound pretty pathetic to you."

He tilted her chin up to look at him. "No, you sounded scared. That's what got my attention. This is what we do. We protect people from stuff like this."

"So, you're like those Ghost Patrol guys?" she asked.

"No!" he said adamantly. "Those guys are idiots. I still don't understand how they ended up with their own TV show about hunting ghosts."

She laughed. "They are pretty stupid."

"Although, there are some legit ghost hunters on TV. It's sometimes hard to tell fact from fiction if you don't already live the life. Come on, let's go check out your room and get you settled in for the night," he said, wrapping an arm around her.

Jessica

Jessica followed Gene across the hall from the kitchen into the library.

He stood in the center and turned in a circle, taking everything in. The interior wall was floor-to-ceiling bookshelves, complete with a rolling ladder to reach the vaulted ceiling. There were hundreds of dust-covered volumes.

It would take her forever to go through them all. She went over to the closest shelves and ran a finger along the bindings as she read some titles. Huckleberry Finn, Tom Sawyer, Treasure Island on one shelf and Farmer's Almanacs on another, books of maps, history, and science on another.

All the books were tidy, the spines of each other perfectly lined up with the ones beside it. Every shelf.

As Jessica walked along the wall, she came to a shelf with no titles on the book. She pulled out the dusty leather-bound book and opened it.

The first page was the family tree. The handwriting changed with each new branch.on

"Judith Martin married George Ferguson. They had two daughters. Edith and Barbara. Barbara married Otto Pike and had a son, Henry, who died at the age of fifteen. Edith married John Witte and had two daughters, Marjory and Beatrice. Edith's eldest daughter, Marjory, never married, but Beatrice married Alan Marr and had one daughter, Jenifer Marr. She married Jack Remington and they had one daughter. Emily Remington," she read to herself, cringing at the sight of her legal name, which she never used. Letting that thought go, she studied the names closely. It was the first time she'd seen her family tree and it was fascinating.

Jessica flipped a little further into the book and read aloud this time

"Planted potatoes in the north forty today. The corn crop is already sprouting and will hopefully be a good crop this year. We are going to need more feed for the cattle to survive the winter. Judith told me today that she's in the family way, so we'll have another baby come February. Edith is hoping for a sister." She replaced the volume and noticed one was sticking out, not neatly lined up with the others. Hesitantly, she pulled it off the shelf and opened the journal.

It was a newer one.

She flipped to the middle and began reading aloud again. *"Grams says trouble's coming. The eclipse last night was an ill omen."*

Gene walked up behind her and looked over her shoulder. His musky smell distracted her.

"She told me to go to the storm shelter before sunset and stay put till

daylight. She won't tell me what's comin'. But she got real mad when I told her I'd just lock up the house."

"How old is that one?" Gene asked.

Jessica flipped to the front. "2010." She felt the color drain from her face.

Gene stepped around to face her.

"I knew Aunt Marge was a little eccentric, but I didn't realize she was crazy."

"What makes you think she's crazy?" he asked.

"Marge was my great aunt. In 2010, she'd have been in her early 80s. But she refers to

'Gram' talking to her." Jessica watched him rub at the back of his neck. She didn't know this hot guy, but he was clearly deep in thought.

Gene

Gene's mind raced. Perhaps Alex was right, and there was a ghost. The house was certainly creepy. There was no evidence of a ghost, but he didn't have his EMF reader either.

He looked back at Jessica, not wanting to freak her out tonight. Perhaps it would be better to discuss Alex's suspicions in the daylight. "Well, maybe she just lived alone too long. You said she was a spinster, and she likely just had an imaginary friend. We can look more into this tomorrow before I fix your car."

Gene glanced out the window. They could pull the car down the road about half a mile and crash there. No one would bother them. It was what they normally did after a job. They only stayed in cheap hotels if the job required more than a few nights' stay. "I should go get Tom. We better hit the road and find somewhere to stay before it's too late."

Jessica looked up at him before sliding the journal back on the shelf. "You don't already have a hotel booked?"

"Nah. We usually fly by the seat of our pants, anyway. Nothing new."

"I'm pretty sure the nearest hotel is over thirty minutes away."

He loved that she cared enough about how far they needed to drive. Something drove him to be honest with her. "It won't be the first time we slept in the car."

"You're gonna sleep in your car tonight?" Jessica asked, wrinkling her nose.

"Yeah, it's no big deal," Gene said.

"Well, it's unconventional, but... why don't you guys stay at the farm with us tonight?" she suggested. "We've got enough beds. And all the doors have locks. So, it's like a free B&B, without the breakfast. We haven't gone shopping yet."

Gene might have a chance to get closer to this woman. He needed to jump on it. "You sure you wouldn't mind? I mean, it'd help us out."

"No, I wouldn't mind," Jessica said, and there was relief stamped all over her pretty face. "I hate to admit I'm a little nervous about staying here the first night, practically alone. Having a few extra bodies around is comforting." She covered her mouth briefly before chuckling. "Live bodies, that is. Who knows what dead bodies are on the property?"

He watched her visibly shudder, but he completely understood. If there was a ghost, the deceased person's body was somewhere on the property—and would need to be found, then salted and burned.

A terrible screeching noise filled the room, and Gene raced for the door.

Jessica was right behind him.

The sound was coming from upstairs.

"Tom!" Gene yelled, taking the stairs two at a time. "Tom!"

His cousin came out of the doorway to the bathroom, as Gene hit the top of the stairs.

"What?" Tom shrugged his broad shoulders, confusion stamped all over his face.

Gene stopped at the top of the stairs, surprised to see his cousin so relaxed. "What is that noise?"

"It's the pipes." Tom said, pointing to the bathroom, "I was going to wash my hands after peeing, if you must know."

"Fine, go wash your filthy hands," he said, waving him back into the bathroom. "But hurry. Jessica offered to let us stay the night. To help her fix her van in the morning."

"Thank you, Jessica. That would help us out. Gene, can you grab my duffle from the trunk?"

"Yup," he said, intending to whirl toward Jessica, but she was standing right behind him. He grabbed her waist to keep from knocking her over. He was so close their lips almost touched.

Her breathing was ragged from racing up the stairs.

Gene didn't miss the desire flash in her eyes and felt the heat of her body.

She quickly stepped out of his embrace and walked into a bedroom. "You can stay in here," she pointed out. "Tom will have the room across the hall."

He followed to the bedroom and leaned against the door frame.

Jessica busied herself pulling the protective sheets off the bed, then moving to uncover the rest of the furniture.

His eyes followed her backside as she moved with purpose. He couldn't be sure if her purpose was to seduce him, but the way she was bending over, at the waist, not the knee, had him thinking it might be an invitation.

Gene strolled into the room and walked up behind her as she tried to fold up the sheet. He touched her biceps to let her know he was there, then slid his hands up to her shoulders and pushed her long silken dark hair out of the way. His fingers kneaded into her stiff muscles as he tried to get her to relax.

Jessica let out a soft moan as her hands dropped to her sides.

He worked a little on her neck before leaning down and whispering in her ear. "You look a little tense," he said, before applying a soft kiss just below her ear.

She moaned again.

He slid a hand around her waist and pulled her back against him.

She was so warm and physically inviting.

The lightbulb in the lamp next to the bed exploded, causing them both to jump back in surprise.

"That's the second time that's happened today," Jessica said, rushing to pick up the pieces.

"Leave it. I'll clean it in the morning. It's not the only light in here. Now, where were we?" Gene reached for her, fully intending to get back to the previous situation. He took her hand in his, slowly pulling her closer.

He was giving her some space. He wasn't a complete asshole, after all. Getting right behind her again, placing his hand in the same spot on her waist, their bodies melted into one another.

They fit so right.

Pop.

The room was instantly enveloped in darkness.

"You gotta be shitting me," Gene huffed. The other lamp's bulb exploded. "You need to get some newer bulbs in these."

She moved around to face him and gently pushed at his chest. "Yeah. I'll get some tomorrow when we get into town to get the parts for my van. I'm sorry you have to get ready in the dark," Jessica said.

"Maybe someone could share their room?" he teased, still standing in front of her, essentially blocking her exit.

"No, Gene. You're a big boy. I'm sure you'll be okay in here. Alone," she said.

She wasn't saying no completely. Just not right now.

"But..."

Jessica flashed a coy smile. "Now, Gene, what kinda girl would I be if I just gave in to you only hours after meeting you?" She took a step forward and caused him to step back toward the door with her hands still on him, the heat searing him.

"You're exactly the kinda lady I like," he said, giving her a roguish smile.

She took another step toward him, and he had to step back again. "No, Gene. I think I need to earn your respect and wait," she said, pushing him through the doorway into the hall.

"Trust me, you have my respect," he said.

Jessica smiled and stepped further into the hallway. Pointing to another closed door across the hall, she said, "That's Tom's room. Make sure he finds it." She turned on her heels, walked to the room next to his, leaned against the frame, and then whispered goodnight before she closed the door on him.

A click let him know she'd locked her door.

A final response to his advances.

Gene stood in the hall, baffled.

This never happened to him.

She was a challenge.

He was always up for a challenge.

He wanted her, and chasing her would be fun.

Tom came out of the bathroom just at that moment. "Got shut down, huh?" his cousin teased.

"No, I just figured what's the rush? I mean, I gotta fix that van in the morning, then check out the 'other' situation," Gene said, heading toward the stairs. "You're in that room," he pointed to where Jessica had indicated. "I'll go grab the bags."

Tom

Tom went toward the little bedroom on the opposite side of the bathroom from Alex's.

He'd just uncovered everything and was shaking off the top covers when Gene tossed his duffle bag to him. "Thanks," he said. He looked at the twin bed, sighing, placing the old sheet he'd just removed at the foot of the bed. He changed into pajama pants and turned off the lights. The springs creaked in protest as he lay on the small bed. At least it was bigger than the backseat of the Mustang.

Tom lay in the small bed, staring up at the ceiling. The room he was in must've been a little girl's room at one time. At six foot five inches, he was a little too long for the twin-sized antique white iron bed frame. He slightly bent his knees to fit on the bed between the head and footboard.

While waiting for Alex to get ready for the night, he'd spread salt around her bed to protect her. He reassured her that as long as she stayed in the circle of salt, the ghost couldn't harm her.

Tom lay there, his mind racing to figure out why a ghost would haunt the place at all. He wanted to get his laptop and do some more research, but he'd left it in the car, and he didn't want to wake the house.

The door to his room creaked open and he reached for his gun beside the bed.

"Tom?" Her voice was so small, that he almost didn't recognize it.

"Alex?" he asked, setting the gun back down and sitting up. "What is it?"

"I'm still scared," she whispered. She wore a pair of pajama shorts and a plain pink tank top that hugged her breasts.

Tom swallowed, and then it dawned on him he was staring. "Come here."

She tiptoed over to the bed.

He pulled back the covers and held them open for her.

She laid down, her back pressed against his bare chest in the tiny bed.

He covered them up, spooning behind her, and wrapped his arms around her.

Alex was trembling, but it could be fear or cold. Jessica had turned down the thermostat to combat the summer heat and humidity.

"I told you that a ghost can't get you in the circle of salt," he whispered.

"I know, but I still can't sleep," she replied.

He smiled.

She'd been in that bed less than an hour, so she hadn't tried to fall asleep. However, Tom was grateful for the excuse to hold her all night. She smelled good and was soft and curvy in all the right places.

Alex's breathing evened out, and the trembling stopped, so she was falling asleep.

He let himself hope, knowing it was the worst thing he could do. The life he lived didn't allow for things like this. What he wouldn't give for a normal life. Could she want someone like him?

*Gene

Gene sighed. The bathroom had no shower curtain, and trying to wash his six-foot-two frame in a claw-foot bathtub wasn't an easy task.

He'd woken up grumpy, and this didn't help. A nice, hot shower in the morning was almost as good as a cup of coffee. Almost. However, when a guy had neither…

Gene stepped out of the bathroom in nothing but a towel, right as Tom entered the hallway.

"Morning," his cousin said, sounding a bit more cheerful than normal. Tom pulled the door to the bedroom closed, but not hard enough to latch it. He passed Gene and headed into the bathroom.

Why was Tom so…happy?

He couldn't resist the curiosity. Gene went to Tom's room, pushing the door open slowly.

Alex was sitting on the edge of the bed, groggily wiping at her eyes.

"Morning, Alex!" Gene smirked. The answer to Tom's mood was before him.

"Morning!" she said, an appealing pink spreading over her cheeks.

He chuckled and headed back to the room he'd slept in. "Lucky Dog!"

Jessica stepped out of her room just as he reached the door.

Her rich dark brown hair was down and tousled, coming to hang just over her breasts. She wore black shorts and a red and black baby doll pajama top that had little Mickey Mouse heads on it.

She stopped dead in her tracks. Her eyes widened, as if she'd just fully woken.

Gene just stood there, wearing only the towel, hair still dripping wet, leaving trails of moisture down his ripped chest. He could only hope his appearance would send her over the edge.

He kept his joy to himself as Jessica pursed her lips together, as if she was trying not to bite her lower lip.

"Did you get some sleep last night?" If he played his cards right, this could go his way. He made his voice deep and gravelly. Intentionally seductive.

"A little," she replied, clearly trying not to betray her attraction.

"I think Alex may have gotten the best night's sleep of all of us," he said with a teasing grin.

Confusion was written in her aquamarine eyes, until the door to Tom's room creaked open and Alex slipped out.

The shorter woman dashed to her room, her head down.

The shock on Jessica's face said everything her silence didn't. Sleeping with his cousin must be completely out of character for Alex.

Jessica obviously tried to play it off, and just shrugged, then headed toward the bathroom.

Tom stepped out of the bathroom just as she came around the banister. His cousin was only half dressed, with pajama pants but no shirt.

Jessica glanced at Gene.

He hadn't moved from the spot where he stood. He smirked as her head went back and forth, as if she was watching the most interesting tennis match.

He and Tom were both shirtless. Their matching tattoos were visible.

He looked down at something he never thought twice about, not since it'd been inked on his left pec. It was as much a part of him as the rest of his body. It was a unicursal hexagram inside a tribal circle of flames, just over his heart. Tom's was the same, style and placement.

The tattoo was a symbol of something vital in their line of work.

He'd wait to see if she brought it up.

Without a word, Jessica went into the bathroom and shut the door, leaving Gene and his cousin in the hallway.

What had she been thinking?

*Alex

Alex quickly changed into a fuchsia sundress with pink flowers embroidered around the bottom, and slid on white sandals. She ran a brush through her hair and grabbed her toothbrush, taking it downstairs to the kitchen. She brushed her teeth before heading out to check on the horses.

She whistled as she circled the corral. The horses raised their heads to look but then went back to eating.

"Oh, I see how it is." Alex smiled.

She checked the bucket of water. It was mostly empty, so she took it to the pump and poured the remaining water into it. It took a few minutes of continuous pumping, but water finally came out. She refilled the bucket and returned it to the corral.

Alex watched her horses and absentmindedly rubbed her right shoulder. It was sore from sleeping on it all night.

"Shoulder hurt?" Tom stepped up behind her. He put his hands on her shoulders and massaged the muscles.

"I shouldn't have slept on my bad shoulder all night, but I was just so comfortable..."

"Your bad shoulder?" Tom asked.

"Yeah, I broke my collarbone a while back. It didn't heal straight, and it still bothers me sometimes," she said, pulling her strap aside so he could see the unevenness in the bone.

He gently ran his fingers over the exposed ridge on her skin and stopped at the slight bump. "You could've rolled over, you know."

She whirled to face him and looked up into his hazel eyes. "It was such a small bed. I didn't want us to fall off. You're so tall, you barely fit as it was."

Tom's thumb stroked her collarbone, sending shivers down her spine. "Well, perhaps tonight we should sleep in your room," he said, looking at his hand, not at her face.

Alex felt another flash of heat running through her body. She hadn't known if they would stay another night, or if Gene would fix the van and they'd hit the road.

She moistened her lips, and Tom leaned down and kissed her softly.

He tasted of cinnamon toothpaste.

**Gene*

In the overly feminine kitchen, Gene sat at the table, feeling a little awkward. He'd scoured the cupboards for anything resembling coffee, only to remember they just moved in.

So he'd pulled out one of the two wire-wound-backed chairs and plopped his ass down. What should he do with himself?

The small round table in front of him was red, and it looked like it belonged in a '50s soda shop. He was a rough-around-the-edged kind of guy who wouldn't be caught dead lounging around in a spot like this. Yet it was cozy, and he could see himself hanging out here, first thing in the morning, a hot cup of coffee in his hands.

"Coffee..." Gene moaned out loud, just another reminder of why he was grumpy.

He'd been listening out for Jessica. Her footsteps were the only ones upstairs because Tom and Alex had already gone outside.

Jessica was still in the bathroom, and her footsteps shifted around in there, before moving over to her bedroom.

Gene tried his damnedest not to picture her getting out of her pajamas and into whatever she'd wear that day. He shook his head hard, trying to clear his thoughts.

You aren't some stupid schoolgirl with a crush. Stop daydreamin'.

He cursed himself. He'd finally made his way upstairs when she'd been in her bedroom for a while. Gene didn't want to rush her, but he needed to get the part for her van, figure out the ghost situation, find out what was going on with the mysterious *'animal attacks'*, and get the hell outta Dodge while he could.

He knocked on her door. "Jessica? Are you about ready to head to town?"

"Almost!" she called.

"All right, I'll meet you downstairs."

"Hold on, I'm just slipping on my shoes. Wait for me."

Gene held his breath when she stepped out of her room.

All her beautiful long hair was pinned up on top of her hair like a curly hat. She had on a turquoise-colored dress that showed off her long legs well. She also wore black high heels that put her only a few inches shorter than his own six-foot-two-inch height.

He offered his arm to help her down the steps.

Outside on the porch, the late morning sun shining down, Gene caught his cousin kissing Alex.

It was weird to see Tom in that position and made him a little uncomfortable, leaving him with knots in his stomach. Happy his little cousin was getting attention, but it was usually him with the girl, not being the one getting shafted, so he hollered down to the other man. "If you two are done making out, we thought we'd head to town."

Jessica stepped up beside him and smacked his stomach with the back of her hand. "You should try to be nice for a change," she scolded.

Again, his breath caught in his throat when he spared her a glance. The sun was hinting at all the different colors in her hair. Not just the shiny brown, but red, honey, and even black strands twisted in her updo. He'd never noticed the multiple shades in a woman's hair before Jessica.

What the fuck is happening to me? I'm thinking like… oh, I don't know!

Gene opened the passenger door of his Mustang for Jessica.

Soon, Tom and Alex joined them.

After letting Alex climb into the back, Jessica slid her fine ass onto the black passenger seat and he closed the door.

Tom walked around the Mustang, apparently ignoring Gene's knowing smirk.

"What?" His cousin shrugged.

Gene waggled his eyebrows.

"Oh! Man, nothing happened," Tom said, clearly irritated at the attention. He climbed into the backseat next to Alex.

"Sure, it didn't." Gene laughed and climbed into the front seat of the car. He started the engine with a low rumble.

Tom just shook his head.

Jessica ran her fingers lovingly over the dashboard of his 1965 Mustang. There was admiration in her pretty face.

"You like my baby?" he asked.

"Yeah," she breathed out. "Last night it was too dark, and I was too upset over Animal to appreciate the beauty."

"Animal?"

"My van. His name is Animal."

Gene nodded.

"But my first love..." She sighed. "My first love was a 1972 Plymouth Duster. I knew that car inside and out. It destroyed me when the ball joints went out."

Gene gaped at the beautiful enigma before him.

What kind of girl is this? I can't imagine she even knows what a ball joint is with the way she dresses.

They drove over an hour and a half into North Platte, the only big town near them with a Walmart and an auto center.

Gene stopped at a restaurant that was still serving brunch. Everyone was hungry and he wasn't the only one in desperate need of coffee.

After eating, they found an automotive store to get the parts Gene needed to fix the van, before they headed off to Walmart so the girls could pick up some things.

Each girl grabbed a cart and headed off in a different direction.

Jessica headed to the grocery department and raced up and down the aisles, Gene on her heels. His cousin had gone with Alex.

He had trouble keeping up with her. "How are you walking so fast in those shoes?" he asked, looking down at her four-inch heels.

Jessica glanced at her shoes and shrugged. "I always wear these. I could outrun you, even in these shoes," she teased.

He shook his head. If she only knew.

Gene felt awkward walking up and down the aisles. He couldn't remember the last time he had been in a grocery store. When they needed necessities, like beer, they stopped at a gas station. This was a piece of normalcy he never thought he'd experience. It was weird. But oddly comforting.

"What should we have for dinner?" Jessica asked.

"It's a little early for dinner, or are you from the south where dinner means lunch and supper means dinner?"

Jessica chuckled. "No, we just had brunch. I mean, what would you like me to cook for dinner tonight?"

"Oh, uh, whatever you like would be fine with me. As long as there's pie for dessert," he flashed a grin.

"Pie, huh? I think I can handle that."

It wasn't long before they had checked out and were on their way back to the farm. Tom helped Alex and Jessica carry in the groceries so the girls could get them put away, and then he and Gene went back to the bar to fix the van.

Gene pulled out the alternator and Tom sat on a curb nearby, trying to balance his laptop on his knees.

His cousin continued to look for more information. "Three bodies ripped to shreds and they think it's a bear. I'm still leaning toward Wendigo. Could be a ghoul, but it really doesn't fit the situation. It shows the land once had Algonquian-speaking natives, known for their beliefs in the Wendigo. Most of the victims were found near a lake. But all in the warmer months. Wendigos are winter monsters by nature."

"I didn't think Wendigos came this far south. So maybe we are looking for a ghoul?" Gene rubbed absentmindedly at his scruffy chin with the back of his left hand. "Well, where is the lake? The nature of a monster means nothing if the setting is right. Haven't we learned that by now?"

Tom jumped up, ran to the vintage hot rod, and grabbed a map of Nebraska. He spread it open on the hood of the Mustang and pointed.

"Why not use your computer for that?" Gene teased.

"Because you always make me get the paper map, anyway. Just saving time."

"Fair. So, how far is the lake?" he asked, wiping his greasy hands on a rag.

Tom sighed. "It's just past the farm."

"Wait, like the girls' farm?"

"Yeah, it looks like it."

"Shit, we gotta get this piece of crap back together and get over there," Gene said, returning to the van and the alternator sitting on the ground.

CHAPTER
SEVEN

*Jessica

Jessica moved the meager contents left in the cupboards to make room for their groceries. The door on the last cupboard on the right kept opening on its own. She'd put something in another cupboard, only to turn around and see that door open again.

She shut it, moved on to the next bag of groceries, turned around, and found it open again.

"Alex!" she hollered. "I think the house has shifted over the years. I can't get this cupboard door to stay closed."

Her best friend entered the kitchen. She'd been in the living room trying to dust off the furniture. Alex shut the troublesome cupboard door. The magnet on the door met with the one inside the cupboard. "What's the big deal? Looks like it's staying in place."

They waited together, still and silent, to see if it opened again. Nothing.

"Maybe you didn't get it closed all the way. I gotta finish cleaning. Let me know if you need something else," Alex said.

Jessica went back to work, too. Once the groceries were all put away, she hand-washed the dishes she'd need to make the pie. It didn't take her long to get the apple pie mixed up and baking. She also made some lemonade and stuck it in the fridge for when the guys came back. It was hot that day and they'd be tired.

Alex came back into the kitchen, washed her hands, and sat at the little table. "Any idea when the guys will be back?" she asked.

"No clue. I hope it doesn't take too long."

Her bestie laughed.

"What?" Jessica asked.

"I can tell you like him. Why don't you just go for it?"

"You know why," she snapped. Jessica had a bad past and didn't want to think about it.

"That was three years ago. Besides, we both know these guys will not stick around forever, so relax and have a little fun," Alex said.

"Like you?" she flashed a smart-ass smile, shifting attention off her.

Her friend waved her off. "Nothing happened. I just spooked myself and couldn't sleep, so he said I could sleep with him."

Jessica couldn't suppress the giggle.

"Not '*sleep with him*' just... sleep," Alex said, rushing her words to show how flustered she was. She made air quotes with her two index fingers.

Her best friend was beet-red by the time Jessica got it together and stopped laughing.

"Why did you freak yourself out?"

"Oh, you know me... creepy old house with creaks and groans. Just felt like someone was watching me."

She sobered. "I know what you mean. Last night, before we went to the bar, I heard you come into my room, but when I looked, you were outside."

Alex visibly shivered. "Agh, don't talk about it! It makes it worse."

"Makes what worse?"

"I think this house has a ghost."

"What?" Jessica shook her head. "No, it doesn't. Alex, you're just being paranoid. And I haven't even watched a scary movie lately. You have always been a scaredy cat. I still can't believe you won't watch Jurassic Park."

"Dinosaurs are scary!" her friend protested. "Besides, there's proof this place is haunted! Tom found a news article where a little girl told everyone the ghost of her grandmother saved her," Alex said.

"Who was the little girl?"

"I don't know. Marjorie something."

"Aunt Marge..." Jessica said, dropping into a kitchen chair.

"You don't think it's true, do you?"

"I don't know what to think. When did Tom look that up?"

"At the bar."

"At the bar? Where was I?" Jessica demanded.

"You were teasing Gene at the pool table."

It was Jessica's turn to be embarrassed. Her face rushed with heat. She was probably as red as Alex.

"Well, I think we should at least get the rest of the furniture uncovered. Then maybe it won't seem so creepy," her bestie said, jumping up. "I'll start upstairs if you want to finish down here. I got the living room done."

"Sounds good. That way, I can keep an eye on dinner. Oh, can you take those new light bulbs up to the room Gene is staying in? Both the lamps' bulbs shattered."

"Still don't think we have a ghost?" Alex teased, before grabbing the package and ascending the stairs.

Jessica put a lasagna together and stuck it in the oven on medium heat to cook for a couple of hours. She could finish it faster, but she didn't know what time the boys would be back.

She wiped down the entire kitchen and rewashed most of the dishes to make sure they were clean. She wiped off countertops and swept and mopped the floor before moving on to the dining room.

The distinctive growl of the Mustang pulling in the drive caught her attention. Jessica stepped out onto the porch and sighed in relief to see Gene pulling in behind Tom, who was driving her van.

She wasn't as attached to the van as she had been to her Duster, but they still needed some transportation.

"You got him running!" She descended the steps, moving toward Gene.

"Well, it still needs a tune-up and an oil change, but I figured it'd be easier to work on here than in the parking lot of the tavern."

"Very true. Thanks for all your help. I appreciate it." Her heart thumped at the idea they might stay longer if her van needed more work. Maybe she could relax her guard with Gene as Alex had suggested. "Can I get you some lemonade?" she asked.

"That sounds great!" he said, flashing a grin that had her heart cantering.

Gene followed Jessica into the kitchen and sat down at the small table.

She felt him watching her move around the kitchen. It made her feel sexy. Jessica added a little wiggle in her hips with each step.

Since her traumatic past, she hadn't wanted to entertain the thought of letting another guy into her life. Even if it was only for a weekend. However, this was fun. She wasn't trying to be a tease, just play.

He seemed like a guy who was used to getting what he wanted. Gene was definitely on the side of arrogant. Hot, but arrogant.

Well, two could play that game.

She'd found a white apron in the pantry that covered the front of her skirt, so she felt like a '50s housewife. Jessica quickly washed her hands and poured them each a cold glass of lemonade. She set the glasses on the table, grabbed a box of shortbread cookies, put some on a plate, and returned to the table.

Gene tracked every move she made.

"What?" she feigned innocence, catching him watching her again.

"Nothin', I just feel like I stepped into an episode of I Love Lucy." He winked.

"I wish I was as beautiful as her, but so glad I'm not that clumsy," Jessica teased.

"Oh, I think you're much more beautiful," Gene said, his green eyes serious and glued to her.

Heat rushed her face all over, and she went for a subject change. "So, do you think my van will last a little longer?"

"Oh yeah, a little work and it will run fine."

"Good, 'cause until Alex buys herself a truck, it's the only vehicle we have," Jessica said.

"Alex's gonna buy a truck?" he asked, arching one of his fine dark eyebrows.

She was getting used to the gesture from him.

"Yeah, she had a little car she sold before we moved so she could buy a truck after we got here."

"I have a hard time picturing her driving a truck," Gene said.

"Don't let the dresses fool you. Alex's a cowgirl at heart. Well, why don't you finish those cookies and I'll go get my sewing machine out of the van and get that shower curtain put together, then you can clean up."

Gene looked down, as if it hadn't occurred to him how dirty he was, but he was covered in sweat, dirt, and grease. "Sounds good," he said, taking another drink of his lemonade.

Jessica headed upstairs to set up her sewing room.

Tom was leaning on the doorframe of the bathroom with his hands in his pockets and his back to her.

"Hey, Tom!" Jessica said. "There's lemonade and cookies downstairs if Gene hasn't eaten them all yet."

Alex stuck her head out of the bathroom. "He better have saved a few, that's bad manners."

Tom laughed, "You don't know my cousin when it comes to sweets."

Jessica smiled after them, then turned to the door behind her. It was the room Gene had slept in last night. She'd debated setting up the machine in her room for now, but it wouldn't matter, since the guys would leave the next day, anyway. She intended to make this small room into her sewing room, so there was no reason to wait.

The headboard of the bed shared a wall with her headboard. The bed was neatly made, which had Jessica arching an eyebrow. She didn't take Gene for the bed-making type and it didn't look like Alex had gotten over here to clean yet.

There was a window on her left and a chest of drawers beyond that. On the opposite wall, past the bed, was a small table with a chair that had most likely been a desk at one point. Gene's green canvas duffle bag was sitting on the desk.

Jessica moved over to the table to set her sewing machine on it. She had her arms full, so she pushed the bag aside to make room to set things down.

The bag fell off the edge of the table next to the bed with a heavy thunk.

She groaned and finished setting her things down. She moved the sewing machine where she wanted, figuring she could plug in the pedal while she was on the floor picking up the contents of Gene's bag.

Jessica pulled the large dark green canvas bag out from under the edge of the bed, but it turned upside down, causing more things to spill out.

Jessica swore, but stared in shock at the things she saw. She'd expected clothes and toiletries, but there were weapons. She gently reached out with shaking hands and picked up the hunting knife.

Was that blood on it?

Jessica dropped the knife into the bag as a silver rod rolled toward her. She gingerly picked it up. It looked heavy but was very light in hand.

Not again!

Her heart thundered in her chest and bile rose in her throat. Intense fear from her past rolled over her, paralyzing her to the floor.

Who are these guys? How could I have let them in my home?

They're homicidal maniacs!

What's wrong with me, thinking this guy is so sexy?

"Jessica?"

Gene stood in the doorway. The scowl on his face made him look dark and menacing.

She scrambled backward, pressing her back to the wall, the rod still in her hand.

He took a step forward.

"Stay back!" she cried.

Gene took another step into the room, "Jessica, what the—"

Jessica pointed the rod at him. "Stay away from me! You will not break me!"

"I'm not going to hurt you," he said, stepping past the end of the bed.

The moment he'd seen the spilled bag, his facial expression changed.

Before she could register what it meant, Tom popped into the doorway, too.

"What's going on?"

Jessica pointed the rod at Tom.

Gene took her moment of distraction to step in, snatching the metal thing from her hand.

She curled up smaller against the wall, trying to get out of his reach.

Alex appeared next to Tom. "Jessica, what happened?"

"Alex, run! He's got a knife!"

Alex looked at Gene and raised an eyebrow.

"This isn't even a knife," he said, sliding it cleanly across his palm for Alex to see. It left no marks on his skin.

It resembled a short sword, but it was cylindrical and was narrower at the tip than the hilt.

Jessica had no doubt it could kill someone if they punctured it through the body, but Gene wasn't threatening anyone while holding it.

She took a deep breath, followed by another, trying her best to bring her heart rate back to a normal beat.

They aren't Justin… They aren't Justin…

"What is it?" Alex asked, starting to calm down.

"It's a serpent sword," Tom said behind her. "It kills certain cryptids."

She looked at him concerned, "What is a cryptid?"

"Things like the Boogy Man, or Loch Ness Monster," Gene said, his voice laced with sarcasm.

That pushed her back over the edge, him not taking the situation seriously.

"What the hell is going on?" Jessica yelled from the floor.

Alex stepped between Jessica and Gene and crouched down in front of her friend. "It's okay, they won't hurt us," she said calmly. "They are hunters. They hunt monsters."

"Monsters? Like what? The things that go bump in the night?" Jessica said incredulously.

"Among other things," Gene said.

She frowned and looked from her best friend to the guy she'd previously been so drawn to. He was still hot, as much as she didn't want to see that. She met Alex's brown eyes.

"It's true," Alex said. "Tom's going to help us with the house's ghost."

Jessica looked up at Gene. "So, you're not going to kill me?"

"I can think of a lot of things I'd like to do to you, but I promise they'd be far more pleasant than killing you," he said, flashing a lustful grin.

Alex smirked.

Jessica grimaced, suddenly embarrassed for assuming the guys were murderers.

"You gonna be all right?" her friend whispered.

Jessica just stared.

You should know I'm not okay. She wanted to scream it out loud, but her past wasn't something she wanted to share with these men she now wanted to call strangers, in her home.

It was a few heartbeats before Alex stood, and retreated from the room, Tom on her heels.

Gene picked up the rest of his gear and threw the bag on the far side of the bed.

Jessica slowly stood up. "I don't know what to say," she whispered. Uncertainty of her feelings about the situation swirled low in her gut.

He dropped onto the end of the squeaky bed and sighed. "It's okay," he grumbled. "That's why we don't tell people what we do for a living. It freaks people out."

Gene ran a hand over his face, and it struck Jessica just how tired he looked.

Why hadn't I noticed before?

She quietly moved next to him on the bed. "Do you seriously hunt monsters?" she asked, disbelief and nerves swarming inside her.

"Yes."

"Why?"

"Because someone has to. We can't just have them running around eating everyone," he said, gesturing with his arm.

"Are there monsters out there that eat people?" Jessica blinked.

"Yeah. Too many different types to count. But we know how to kill most of them. So, don't worry, I won't let them get you."

"How long have you been... um... hunting?"

Did she want to know the answer?

"I've been hunting longer than Tom. He got lucky and has only been in the life a few years. I feel like I have always been hunting. That or *been* hunted."

A sob caught in her throat. The sudden emotion was a surprise, but she felt...so much...for him in that moment. He looked so sad. Resigned. Hot tears rolled down her cheeks.

Gene gently wiped the tears away. "It's okay. It's the life I have. I wouldn't change it. I can't imagine what would've happened to all the people I've saved in the past if I had never picked up a blade," he said. He leaned in slowly—as if giving her an out—his soft, full lips pressing against hers.

Jessica was hesitant. Something deep in her called out to him, wanting the closeness of a man, but her immediate response was to push him away.

Her desire to taste him won, and she moved in, parted her lips, and returned the kiss. She slowly opened her eyes, when Gene pulled back.

He smiled at her and wiped something from her chin. He was still all dirty. He moved in for another kiss.

Without letting herself think about it, Jessica slid her fingers into his dark brown hair. There wasn't enough to get a grip on, but she still delved into the richness.

His hair was soft, even though it was moist with sweat and grime from being under the hood of her van. Her nails gently scraped his scalp and their lips parted as their tongues did a hot dance.

Jessica was sitting beside him, turned at an awkward angle.

His right hand slid down her thigh, grazing the fabric of her dress.

Before she could breathe, he slipped his hand under her knees and scooped her onto his lap.

She laughed and slid her hand from his hair to knead his neck, and their kisses intensified.

His hand navigated up the hem of her dress, caressing her skin.

Within moments, she was breathless and needed to break away to bring air back into her lungs. Taking a deep breath, she inhaled the smell of him. His masculine scent, oil, dirt, and sweat.

It was oddly intoxicating.

It only took a moment for her senses to come back, and she panicked.

This was how she ended up with Justin.

She couldn't go down that dark road again, no matter how hot the guy was. She scurried off his lap, fleeing his room.

"What's wrong, darlin'? I already told you I'm not a homicidal maniac," Gene's voice followed, but she didn't stop.

CHAPTER
EIGHT

Jessica

Jessica sat at her dressing table; her face buried in her hands, dying from embarrassment. She took a big breath, she had to get it together.

She glanced up, looking at the stranger in the mirror. Her face was smudged with dirt and grime, her lips were slightly swollen from his kisses. Her cheeks were flushed red with passion and streaked from her tears.

This wasn't like her.

Shame made her avert her eyes from her reflection, and she looked down. There was grease on her dress.

Jessica growled. The dress was ruined. She quickly stood and pulled the dress off, hoping to get it to the laundry room before the stain set. When she went to the closet—where she had a few dresses hanging—her bedroom door opened.

"What was tha..." Gene said, but he didn't finish his sentence. His Adam's apple bobbed with an audible swallow.

She wore a turquoise lace bra, almost the same color as her dress, and a white silk bloomers. She couldn't have been more exposed if she was naked. Her cheeks seared, and she could barely do anything but stare. She hadn't expected him to follow. Let alone, he hadn't knocked before he'd burst into her room. "My…uh, my…dress," she held up the soft fabric, showing him the mark of grease.

"Piece of cake. I can get that out. I know ways to remove just about any stain." Gene moved away from the doorway, his hand outstretched. He took the dress and examined the mess he'd caused. "I just need some shampoo. But… your face is far dirtier than your dress," he whispered and reached for her cheek.

But not nearly as dirty as our thoughts.

A new rush of heat filled her torso, and she prayed she wasn't bright red. She also hoped he couldn't read her mind.

He slid a soft caress from her cheekbone down to her lips. "I'm sorry if I scared you. As I said, we rarely share what we do with other people. This is what happens. But since your van is fixed now, we can hit the road right away."

"Oh, uh… thank you. But…" Jessica didn't want him to leave. She couldn't explain why, but she needed him to stay a while longer. "The ghost!"

"Huh?" Gene blinked.

"We need you to figure out if we have a ghost, and, um… hunt it."

"So you don't want us to leave yet?" He took a step closer to her, their bodies just inches apart.

"I made lasagna." She was fumbling for a reason to keep him there.

"Jessica," he whispered, closing the remaining distance between them. "Are you asking us to stay another night?"

"Yes," she breathed, unable to deny her desire for him further.

His left hand snaked around her waist, pulling her into his body, where she fit far too nicely.

Without waiting another moment, Gene stole another kiss, and her breath.

Her knees buckled under her. Her skin erupted in goosebumps as he ran his fingers up her back.

"Gene, are you in here?" Tom's voice came through the door to Jessica's room.

"Not now Tom!" His voice was rough, chastising his cousin.

His cousin didn't say another word. However, it sounded like he'd set something down by the door and headed back downstairs.

Once again, Jessica had come to her senses. She pushed at Gene's rock-hard chest, moving him toward the door. "Please," she pleaded. "Go take a shower before we both end up completely dirty." She got him to the door and opened it one sentence.

He sighed, defeated, and headed to the bathroom with a disappointed nod.

Gene's kisses were as hot as he was. His touch set her on fire from the inside out, but Jessica wasn't ready to go there.

She just couldn't.

*Tom

Alex was in the kitchen when Tom came back downstairs. She was pulling a dish out of the oven and placing another tray in.

"Smells good," he said, taking a seat at the small table.

"Yeah, Jessica's an excellent cook," she said. She went to the fridge and grabbed a beer for Tom and a bottle of wine.

"So how long till we eat?" he asked.

"Just waiting for Jessica and Gene to come down," she said, sitting across from him and handing him the opened bottle.

"Uh... They may be awhile," he said awkwardly.

"Why's that?" Alex asked, and then understanding dawned on her pretty face. "Oh! Well, good for her."

Her reaction made him sit back, leaning away from the table. "Why do you say that?"

"Oh, it's just..." Alex's expression again spoke for her. She was debating on what to reveal about her best friend. "A few years ago, Jessica met this guy," she continued after a few heartbeats, and without Tom prompting her. "They seemed so perfect together, had the same interests and everything. He was an antique dealer and traveled a lot for work. They'd been dating for almost a year when she got suspicious of some of his dealings. She started checking into him and found out that he was selling stuff on the black market."

"What kind of stuff?"

"Body parts," she spat, as if disgusted. "Jessica found boxes with these weird symbols on them and when she opened one, there was a bloody heart inside." Alex visibly shivered.

Tom leaned forward a little in his chair. "What did the symbols look like?"

"I don't know. I didn't see them. Wait, you don't think they might be your kind of thing, do you?"

"Could be. There are people out there who deal in magical items. Most of them are just fortune hunters, and they aren't even sure what they've actually been dealing with, but some of those people are dangerous. Jessica's lucky she figured it out before she got hurt," Tom said.

"She didn't." She looked at the wine bottle. "Jessica confronted him, and he beat her within an inch of her life. He threatened to kill her if she ever told anyone. He purposely crashed his car to hide the beating. Cops never caught him. As soon as she was out of the hospital, she ran away from Portland and asked me to join her and start over in a new state, before finding out about this house. It was rough on her. She's never really trusted any guy since."

"So, when she found the weapons..." Tom said, understanding now. He cursed. His poor cousin.

"Exactly."

"Well, Gene and I have to lie a lot to do what we do, but once someone knows about our jobs, then there isn't much point in trying to hide things. Sometimes what you don't know can get you killed."

"So why not tell everyone?" Alex asked.

"Because then everyone would panic. And if you could happily live the rest of your life not knowing about these things, wouldn't you?"

"Can you teach me?" she asked, biting her full bottom lip, as if she was nervous.

He chastised himself to concentrate on what she was asking, and not recalling the taste of those lips moving under his. "Teach you what?"

"To protect myself," she said, her voice sincere.

Tom smiled. "Sure."

Jessica stepped through the door of the kitchen.

Tom and Alex looked up, collectively surprised.

He again yelled at himself for not hearing her. What a hunter he was. He shouldn't let his guard down. However, Alex and Jessica were far from just another job.

Jessica changed into a short black dress with black knee-length leggings underneath. She was barefooted and had removed her makeup, leaving her features looking softer than they did with the eye makeup.

She went straight to the oven and checked the French bread. "Good, the butter's all melty." She grabbed a plate out of the cupboard and took it into the dining room.

Alex glanced at Tom. "I thought she'd be in a better mood."

"I don't think they—" he cleared his throat when Jessica came back into the kitchen.

"Dinner's ready, if you guys want to wash up," she said, picking up the tray of lasagna.

"Where's Gene?" Alex asked.

"He took a quick shower. He should be down shortly," her friend said, heading back to the table.

Alex and Tom exchanged a look.

The dining room table could easily seat ten, but Tom didn't

want to be far from Alex. He reached for the chair next to hers, returning her smile when their eyes met.

Jessica was avoiding their gazes, and it didn't escape him that there was an awkwardness in the air. He didn't like it.

Tom liked these two, and they were quickly becoming more than just friends—well, at least Alex was for him, and there was no shocker that his cousin had a thing for Jessica. They were good for each other. At least until now. He wasn't sure what had transpired upstairs.

Gene came downstairs and joined them in the dining room. He reached for the chair next to Jessica, across from Tom and Alex. "You didn't have to wait for me."

"Yes, we did," Tom said.

"It's good etiquette," Alex said.

"Please help yourself," Jessica said. Her gesture to the pan of food was stiff, as was her posture, like she didn't want to be so close to his cousin.

Tom's hunger won over his frustrations about the other would-be couple. He reached for the spoon, and scooped out lasagna, while Alex opened the bread.

Jessica handed Gene a bowl of freshly steamed asparagus.

After a few minutes of more awkward silence, his cousin cleared his throat. "Do you girls know where there's a lake around here?"

"A lake?" Jessica asked, "No, why? Did you want to go swimming?"

"Ah no," Tom sighed. "We think there may be trouble near this lake."

"And it's close to here?" Alex asked.

Gene nodded.

"Great!" Alex said, her voice dripping with sarcasm. "We moved into a death trap."

Tom squeezed her hand. "We're not even sure there's something there yet. Gene and I need to go to town tomorrow and do some more digging."

"So, you're going to stick around for a few more days?" she asked, with a mischievous grin.

"I wasn't planning on leaving until we found your ghost. But now we have something a bit more worrisome to think about first. I've got to get to my computer and start researching," he said. He was driven to make sure these ladies were safe. Also, grabbing his computer would get him away from the weird tension in the dining room.

"Sit your butt down," Jessica chastised. "Dinner first."

Alex

"What happened?" Alex asked.

After dinner, she and her bestie went into the kitchen to do the dishes while the guys went to the living room to do some more research.

"Huh?" Jessica said with obvious distraction. She wasn't paying attention while she dried a plate Alex had just washed.

"Tom said you and Gene were... um... getting to know each other. Then a few minutes later you were down here, alone, and not smiling."

"I don't want to talk about it," her friend grumbled.

"I don't get it. I thought you were into him," she complained.

"I am. That's the *problem*," Jessica said, her slender shoulders caving in.

Alex could feel her friend's despair. She set the dish she was washing down in the rinse pile. "How is that a problem?"

"Because it'll never work."

"What will never work? I'm pretty sure he's good to go on this," she teased, trying to make her bestie smile. Regret washed over her when their eyes met.

Jessica had tears in her eyes.

"Jessica, what is it?" Alex asked, frowning.

"That stupid fortune teller was right. I'm cursed," she said. She slunk away from the double farm sinks, going to sit at the small red table and setting the dish she was drying in front of her.

"What the heck are you talking about?"

"Do you remember Laurie's 18th birthday party?" Jessica's voice was desperate.

She nodded. "Vaguely," Alex said.

"Do you remember the fortune teller there?"

"Yeah, she told me something stupid about a mountain changing my life."

Jessica cocked her head to one side, frowning. "Yeah, well, I didn't think much about what she said either, until Justin."

"What do you mean?" Alex asked, leaning against the counter.

"She said that I'd meet my soulmate, and we'd have this instant connection that bonded us together, but there would be something dark that would tear us apart."

"And you think that was Justin?" She made a face.

"It made sense. At least it used to. I thought we were going to get married. I loved him so much, and then I found out what he was doing and..." Her friend trailed off in tears.

Alex sat across from her and reached out for her hands. "Jessica, fortune tellers aren't real. Especially ones that come to teenage girls' birthday parties. And yes, Justin was scary, but that just means he wasn't your soulmate. Your soulmate is someone who would die for you, not someone who threatens to kill you."

"But part of her predictions *have* come true. She said I'd be my own boss someday and be doing something I love. That's happened. I want to accept it was hokey, but there was some truth to the fortune teller."

"That's such an open-ended story. You could take that ten different ways," Alex said, squeezing her hands.

"You think so?" Jessica said, tugging one free, and wiping her tears away.

"Of course I do. Lots of people find something they love to do and then turn it into a career. Besides, in all the years I worked for the forest service, do you ever recall a mountain that changed my life?" she said, again trying to get her friend to smile.

Jessica did smile, but it was halfhearted.

"Is that what's holding you back with Gene?" she asked, "Do you think you already missed your chance?"

Her friend just nodded.

"Well, don't let it stop you with Gene. Gene probably isn't the one, but that doesn't mean you can't relax and have a little fun," Alex said, smiling again.

"You think so?" Jessica asked.

"They aren't the *'stick around and settle down'* kind of guys. But from what I can tell, they both have good hearts. Think about it, they save people all the time."

"I guess you're right. I feel like I should trust him, even though I just found out he'd lied to us about his work." Her bestie let out a long sigh. "It was like he'd been protecting me from the nightmare that is his life."

"Maybe? Now, would you just go talk to him?" Alex said, pulling Jessica out of her chair.

Her friend picked up her unfinished glass of wine and drained it before she walked toward the living room, and Gene.

CHAPTER
NINE

Jessica

Jessica took a deep breath as she stepped into the living room. This was it. She'd either go for it, learn to open herself up again, or chicken out, letting Justin win again.

The cousins sat beside each other on the antique couch that was once likely a pretty peach color. They were both leaning in to read something on the laptop screen.

Jessica watched for a moment to see if Gene would look up, but he seemed nose-deep in his investigation, so she lost her nerve and whirled to walk out. There were boxes to unpack.

She didn't want to distract him from his... what had they called it?

Oh, yeah, hunting.

Gene finally looked up, as she cut through the corner of the living room and headed for the stairs. He rushed to his feet and caught up to her before she reached the third step. He grabbed her forearm, gently stopping her. "Jessica?" he asked, curiosity rich in voice timbre voice.

She looked down and melted on the spot.

Before, his eyes had been filled with lust, but now, as he gazed up at her, there was genuine concern creasing his brow. "Is everything okay?" he asked gently, letting his hand slip from her forearm to her hand.

Jessica glanced at Tom, who was pretending not to notice them as he worked on his computer.

She looked back at Gene, squeezed his hand, and continued heading up the stairs, staying silent as she led him to her room. She dropped his hand and closed the door behind them.

As Gene stood in the center of the room, his face stamped with confusion, Jessica moved to the dresser where her iPhone had been charging.

She pulled up her music and selected her "Greatest Hits of Mullet Rock". It was her guilty pleasure, and she rarely played the songs around Alex. It was classic rock and a few power ballads.

Jessica could sing them like no one's business and felt the words in her soul. She had a feeling Gene would appreciate it. She also needed something to block the noise she was no doubt about to make. She tried not to giggle when the first song started.

Jessica stepped up to Gene as the slow, soft notes started. "Dance with me," she asked, breathlessly.

He nodded and pulled her close.

They moved in a small circle, her head on his shoulder.

Shock rushed up when he started singing along quietly, like he was embarrassed.

Her favorite song by *Air Supply* was playing. '*All Out of Love*'. Jessica took over, keeping her head on his shoulder.

As the chorus began, she looked up into his green eyes and they sang to each other.

She started giggling but was silenced when Gene cupped her cheek and kissed her softly.

Since her hands were already behind his head, it was easy for her fingers to find their way into his hair.

Justin, her ex-boyfriend, had always had a buzz cut, much to her protest, since she loved having her fingers entrapped in a man's locks.

She banished the thought of her ex. He didn't belong in this room at this moment, and he already had too much of her headspace. Jessica needed to banish him. She wrapped her fingers in Gene's hair. She couldn't help herself. His hair was so soft. Now it was clean from his shower.

Even better.

He helped to part her lips so their tongues could keep up the dance their bodies had started. His hands easily found the hem of her very short dress and slipped under to find the skin of her lower back. His fingertips swirled around, making goosebumps erupt.

Jessica waited for Gene to pull the dress off, but when he didn't; she broke the kiss and in one swift movement, had the T-shirt-like dress over her head and on the floor.

The song shifted and began playing '*Hot Blooded*'. It was as if her playlist knew what to choose next.

She tried not to listen to the words as she pulled Gene's olive-green button-up shirt down his arms to join her dress on the floor. Jessica ran her hands over his defined biceps.

He grabbed the bottom of his black T-shirt and pulled it over his head, baring his rock-hard chest to her.

She ran her fingers down the smooth skin covering his abs. They were firm and warm, like steel. Jessica giggled at the thought. *Abs of steel.*

She trailed her fingers lower to undo the buckle of his black leather belt. She could see the strain of the fabric against his erection.

His breath came out in a hiss, as her knuckles grazed the tight fabric before she undid the top button.

She expected to find him commando as she unzipped his jeans; it surprised her to find boxer briefs. She ran her tongue over her lips in anticipation.

Before Jessica moved any further, he brought her back up straight to assault her lips again.

As the kisses intensified and the heat built up, Gene walked her backward toward the bed.

Jessica almost lost her balance when the back of her legs hit the mattress. She laughed as she plopped down onto the squeaky bed.

He gently pushed her back, hooking his thumbs into the waistband of her black leggings, and removed them. He looked at her hungrily as he tossed the leggings over his shoulder to have them land on the pile with the other clothes.

She propped herself up on her elbows as she watched him drop his pants and boxers on the floor.

It was comical, the look on his face as he did so. He was grinning like a cat that got the canary.

Gene put one knee on the bed, prepared to straddle her. When the bed made a horrendous squeaking noise, he smiled devilishly, but the sound made Jessica's heart flutter.

"Yeah, this isn't going to work," she said, trying to push him off and sit up.

He smiled. "If the bed's a-rockin', don't come a-knockin'."

Jessica laughed but shook her head. "If I have any idea how loud this adventure is going to be, we don't need to be letting Alex and Tom know all about it. The best thing about having sex on a squeaky bed is the skill to do everything the slow way so that the bed doesn't squeak. I want to see you try that."

Gene offered her his hand and helped her to her feet, pulling her against him. "I accept that challenge," he said with a grin. "But you're right, that's for another time." He reached around her, grabbing the comforter on the bed and pulling it to the floor.

It wasn't ideal, as sex on the floor always gave her a backache, but a squeaky bed, was not the best way to stay quiet.

One thing she and Alex had prided themselves on was their etiquette. Proper etiquette was not to let your friends hear you having wild, passionate sex.

Jessica laughed as she contemplated Alex and Tom downstairs

looking up at the ceiling with all the noise. She shook the thought from her head and gestured for Gene to hit the floor.

"Ladies first," he said with a wicked grin.

She gave him a gentle push. "Not this time, cowboy," she cooed with a bit of seduction.

Gene's eyes widened in anticipation. He lay down on the comforter and tucked his hands behind his head.

Jessica stood above him in just her turquoise lace bra and panties. Alex was right, this guy wasn't '*the one*', her soulmate, so she might as well enjoy herself. She observed his face as she took a moment to pull every bobby pin out of her hair and shake her glorious long hair out.

Her hair was long enough and thick enough that when over the front of her shoulders, it completely covered her breasts. She reached behind her back and unhooked her bra, letting the fabric drop at her feet. Poor Gene, he still didn't quite get to see what he had been holding his breath for.

A new song started on her playlist. '*Black Velvet*' by Alannah Myles. She felt the seduction in the song. Jessica tried not to sing along, but without conscious thought, her hips swayed back and forth ever so slightly to the beat of the music.

She stepped onto the comforter, putting one foot on either side of Gene's hips.

He trailed his eyes from her thigh to her hip, across to her smooth stomach. They lingered a moment longer at the underside of her breast, then finally rested on her eyes.

Jessica moved seductively to fully straddle him, her knees now on the ground, gently squeezing his hip bones. Even though she still wore her scrap of lace panties, she hovered just a breath away from his hard shaft, absolutely teasing him.

She leaned down to kiss him, her long hair spilling around them both. She pressed her bare breasts against his rock-hard chest.

Gene grabbed her hips, gently digging his fingers into the soft flesh.

She was reaching her goal, hoping to drive him crazy. This was one night she was sure he would never forget. As Jessica kissed him, she gently rocked her body, teasing him even further.

Without warning, he flipped them over, landing Jessica hard on her back. It took her a moment to catch her breath, it was so unexpected.

Gene slid down her body ever so slightly, just enough to capture her right breast in his waiting mouth.

The talent he had with his tongue sent heat pooling between her legs.

He growled slightly under his breath, causing Jessica to gasp. When he released her, he lifted ever so slightly to look at her face.

"Can you smell it Jessica, can you smell the desire we're filling this room with?"

She'd never understood the need for pillow talk. Who cared if she could smell their sex?

She just wanted to get to it. She said nothing, just nodded.

He was obviously satisfied with her response, because he took a moment to devour her left breast, making sure it did not feel unloved.

Jessica arched her back in response to his attack.

Gene trailed kisses down her rib cage, to her hipbone, where she tried so hard not to laugh.

She wasn't necessarily ticklish, but she had never been kissed like that before.

He grabbed the scrap of lace with his teeth and gently pulled at it like he was trying to remove it. Ever the jokester, but she loved it.

Jessica laughed, her whole body shaking with joy. She giggled, and he slipped his thumbs under the waistband. In one swift movement, he slipped her panties off and tossed them aside.

Gene moved back up, so ready to fill her body with his own.

She was ready for him.

Jessica reached up for him, delving her fingers back into his soft hair, pulling him down for a kiss. He fit so perfectly against her. She wrapped her long legs around his hips, trying to draw him in.

She felt the soft tip of his erection press against her core. She lifted her hips, pushing him in so slightly. Rather than continue to tease her, Gene surged deep, filling her completely.

He started a delicious rhythm that made Jessica purr in delight. However, after a moment, she stopped him.

"What's wrong?" he asked as she pushed gently at his chest.

"Nothing," she smiled wickedly. "Just switching things up. It's my turn. On your back, hunter." Jessica hovered just above him, slowly taking him into her, inch by wonderful inch. Even though the song was not the one currently playing, she had 'Slow Ride' by Foghat playing in her head.

Alex had taught her well how to ride a horse, and she put her lessons to good use. She rode him with a skill she hadn't realized she had. She used muscles she hadn't used in this aspect in so long.

He felt so good inside her, and so different from him being on top. Who was enjoying it more?

The look on his face, Gene was definitely in heaven. His hands had been behind his head when they started, then moved to her hips to help with the rhythm. Her slow pace didn't last long, and she moved faster and faster, her body began the delicious build-up.

Gene

Gene propped himself up on his elbows so he could watch her face. At that moment, he wanted more. Something he'd never wanted to do before.

He pushed himself up into an almost sitting position, making it so he could wrap his arms around her. It was so close and intimate. He had never been there before.

This didn't feel like his normal—just sex. This was becoming too much.

So, he repositioned them, getting Jessica back underneath him. He had to change his mood. Balking to himself about being a patsy. He was Gene *'freakin'* Priest. He didn't do emotional sex.

He let the raw sexual desire take over as his rhythm went deeper and faster.

Jessica bit her lower lip to keep from crying out. Her body tightened around him, and her orgasm rocked her.

He was close, too.

She squeezed all her lower muscles, tightening her legs around his hips, as he pushed hard and deep until his own release came.

He collapsed, trying so hard not to crush Jessica. They lay there for several minutes, each of them trying to catch their breath.

It wasn't easy with her fingertips slowly and methodically trailing up and down his back, showing him a tenderness he wasn't used to.

Gooseflesh covering his suddenly sensitive skin. Gene propped himself up on his elbow and kissed Jessica again. "I guess we better get cleaned up," he said.

She smiled and nodded.

He made it to his feet and offered Jessica a hand. He pulled her to her feet then and scooped up the comforter. He wrapped the comforter around his shoulders, then wrapped his arms around Jessica, covering them both as they snuck off to the bathroom.

A short time later, Gene lay on his stomach, his hands tucked underneath the pillow and his head completely content.

Jessica was beside him, on her back with her hair fanned around the pillow.

He couldn't believe how his night was ending. He'd had a delicious dinner and an unexpected dessert…

Dessert!

He'd totally forgotten!

"Hey, Jessica? What about pie?"

CHAPTER
TEN

Alex

Alex finished up the dishes. She refilled her wine glass and grabbed another beer for Tom. She went into the living room with a little extra swish in her hips to get his attention. It didn't work.

He didn't even look up from the laptop as she sauntered over.

Tom was sitting in the middle of the couch, working on his laptop, which was resting on the coffee table. He looked uncomfortable, all bent over, but he barely glanced at the beer when she set it down.

She sat next to him, looking over his shoulder at the screen. "Whatcha workin' on?" Alex asked.

"I'm trying to find out if there's a common connection between the victims or if they were all just found in the same place," he said. He closed one tab on the computer and opened another.

Alex watched for a few minutes, trying to follow along, but Tom seemed to be deep in thought on it and she didn't want to interrupt by asking a lot of questions.

He quickly lost her as he skimmed through multiple articles and county records.

She leaned back on the couch and admired his broad shoulders as she sipped wine.

Tom stretched.

His back probably hurt from bending over the coffee table. The furniture was old, and back then, they didn't design furniture for someone as tall as he was.

Alex hated to admit it, but she was getting bored watching him work.

Tom didn't explain any of his findings or keep her informed of whatever he was gathering. He probably wasn't trying to be malicious; he was just really focused on what he was doing.

Her head got heavy, and at some point, she tilted back into the couch and closed her eyes.

Tom pushed some hair back away from Alex's face, bringing her back to consciousness.

"Did I fall asleep?" she whispered.

He took the empty wineglass from her hands and set it next to his computer. "It's okay. I'm sorry, I didn't realize I was working so long."

She glanced at her watch. It'd been a couple of hours. She must've drifted off after all.

"Time always seemed to slip away from me when I'm on the job. Let's get you upstairs." He slipped a well-muscled arm under her knees, the other around her waist, and stood up with surprising ease. He started toward the stairs.

"You don't have to carry me," Alex said. Her body flushed with embarrassment, and she couldn't shake the self-consciousness washing over her. "I know I'm not exactly a skinny supermodel. I'm solid, with more muscle than most girls."

"I know I don't have to carry you. But I've always wanted to carry a beautiful woman up an antique flight of stairs," he said, with a smirk on his handsome face.

"Like Rhett Butler."

"Who?" Tom asked.

"'*Gone With The Wind*'?" Alex blinked. Could he really not

know about the classic movie? Jessica had made her watch it since it was her bestie's favorite movie.

That was the only scene Alex could remember, Rhett scooping up Scarlet and carrying her up the grand flight of stairs.

"Never seen it."

He wasn't even winded, and it was impressive. He wasn't having any trouble carrying her. Then again, he was a big guy. Tom stood a foot taller than her when she wasn't wearing shoes, with broad shoulders and muscular arms.

The door to Jessica's room was closed, and it seemed quiet inside, so Alex assumed Gene and Jessica were asleep.

Tom sat her on the purple comforter spread across the bed in her room and kissed her cheek. "I'll let you get changed. I'm going to have a shower," he said.

Alex watched him leave, despite the fact that she didn't want him to. Too late, she watched him exit the door. Uncertainty churned in her stomach. She needed to take her own advice and have fun, like she'd told Jessica.

Is that what she truly wanted?

Or was it that she just didn't want to be alone?

Tom went to his room briefly, exiting with a toothbrush and pajama pants in his grip.

She tried not to stalk, but he was visible in the bathroom, since he hadn't closed the door.

He started the noisy shower, and let it heat up while he brushed his teeth. Tom adjusted the shower curtain to block most of the water.

Since Jessica hadn't made the wrap-around curtain yet, they were just making do with the one Alex had found and hung when she was cleaning.

When he turned to shut the door, Alex took a step back into her room, hoping he hadn't seen her.

What am I doing? Being a Peeping Tom?

She'd never been as bold as her dearest friend. She was

usually the wallflower in most social situations unless Jessica pulled her into a crowd.

However, tonight, Alex found a bravery she'd never had before. She stripped off her clothes, grabbed a soft satin robe from her room, and headed to the occupied bathroom.

She hoped the door wasn't locked.

Tom

The hot water felt good on his tired back. Tom was looking forward to stretching out next to Alex in the bigger bed.

I hope she is still all right with sharing her bed.

At first, he didn't hear the bathroom door open and close again. There was a subtle noise he wrote off to being in a big, old house. He wiped his eyes after rinsing his shoulder-length hair out.

Alex stepped into the shower with him.

They didn't speak, but they did make eye contact, and he offered a smile.

She seemed a little awkward like she wasn't sure what she was doing.

Well, she was most certainly welcome in the shower with him.

Tom pulled her into his arms and kissed her deeply. He turned them around so she could be under the hot water.

Alex tilted her head back and rinsed her hair while he trailed kisses along her neck, exploring her backside with both hands.

There was no denying how aroused he was.

She reached between them and gripped his shaft.

He braced himself in the tub as she massaged him. If she didn't stop, he'd come all over her hands, and he didn't want to climax that way. He pulled her to him, grinding against her, trying to connect their most sensitive spots. Their height difference was too much.

Without a word, Tom threw back the small shower curtain, stepped out of the tub, and scooped her up in his arms. He opened the door and carried her down the hall, both of them naked and dripping wet.

He used his foot to close her door and laid her out on the bed. Tom took a moment to study her glorious body, all its curves and dips. This was one night he wanted to remember forever, one night to get him through the endless nights alone.

Tom joined her on the bed, leaning over her, resting all his weight on his arms, on either side of her. His kisses were deep and urgent. He moved slowly down her body, kissing Alex's left ear, the pulse at her neck, the curve of her collarbone.

He tenderly cupped her right breast, rolling the dark pink nub between his thumb and forefinger. He glanced into her gorgeous face.

Alex's tempting tongue was moistening her dry lips, before she bit the bottom one.

He loved that her nipples and lips were almost the same color. Tom took the right one into his mouth, enjoying the softness of it against his tongue, the slightly salty taste it left there. Finally releasing it, the other breast begged for the same full attention.

She arched her back as he teased her with his teeth.

Taking his sweet time, Tom moved lower, nipping at her ribcage, licking off the water on her stomach, making her giggle before moving lower, sampling every inch of her olive skin.

Alex gasped as his tongue danced around her most intimate spot. He found what he sought, the hooded button throbbing for his touch.

He worked her until she was right on the cusp of exploding, flicking, sucking, and circling until she was bent over so far he thought she'd break her back.

She whimpered, and it was little more than a plea for sweet release.

He wanted to be inside her so they climax together. However, Tom wasn't selfish. He could give her more. Flicking faster, he brought his forefinger to her entrance and circled the soft skin, not moving in, only around.

"Tom!" Alex gasped, telling him he was doing right by her.

Not stopping his assault on her swollen clit with his tongue, he slipped his finger inside her, palm up, to curl his finger ever against her g-spot. He gently tapped that quivering flesh.

She felt so close. He slid another finger inside and applied a little more pressure.

Alex's body went ridged, and she screamed in ecstasy.

He'd pushed her over the edge.

Tom didn't want to wait anymore. He wanted her.

While her body continued to shudder from aftershocks, he leaned back, knocked her knees apart, and thrust deep. He closed his eyes as sensations washed over him; his cock felt the tightness of her still-climaxing muscles around him.

Alex wrapped her legs around him.

He moved in and out slowly, letting her ride the pleasure as long it lasted.

After a few moments, she let him know without words that she wanted more. She lifted her hips with each thrust, matching his rhythm, causing his breathing to become as ragged as hers.

Tom moved faster and deeper, until he felt her body spasm around him a second time. He wanted to join her in shared bliss; he was close, too. He thrust as deep as her body allowed, and his balls met with her warm skin over and over.

He was close.

So close.

Two more times of plunging into her soft body was all it took. With a grunt, he released himself into her.

He wanted to fall forward; his arms were so tired from holding his frame up, but he didn't want to crush her. Nor did Tom want to leave the heat of her body. He grabbed her close, and rolled her to side, separating their bodies. He collapsed into the bed with a contented sigh. Flat on his back, he felt peace he hadn't had in a very long time.

He smiled. Tom tilted his head so he could see Alex's face, which was turned his way. "I think we left the shower running," he breathed out.

She giggled. "We could both use another shower now."

He moved into her, kissing the edge of her closest breast, then pushed himself up into a sitting position, before finally standing up. Tom held out a hand to her; she took it.

In the hallway, Tom didn't miss Alex looking at Jessica's door and he could almost feel her self-consciousness. He just wanted to grab her up and make her feel better. Then he'd kiss her and take her again. "Trust me, they're asleep," he whispered.

They hurried back to the bathroom, and Alex stepped into the shower first.

Tom stepped in behind her and grabbed the bottle of shampoo. The hot water felt good. He squirted some in his hands and massaged it into her hair.

Alex moaned in pleasure.

He used the extra suds to wash off her body.

She rinsed off and they switched places. She reached up and kissed him. "That was the sexiest thing anyone has ever done for me," she said.

Tom smiled. He'd never washed someone else's hair, but he just wanted to keep his hands on her as long as possible. He was the type of guy who'd never get a chance to settle down, no matter how much he wanted to. However, this girl was making him feel like maybe he could find a way. Or at least made him want to. "Why don't you dry off while I finish and then we can go to bed?"

Alex stepped out of the tub. She wrapped herself in a short satin robe she'd worn into the bathroom.

Tom rinsed and turned off the shower. He dried quickly and slipped on his pajama pants. He took Alex's hand as they walked back to her room. He couldn't stop touching her.

He and Gene wouldn't be there much longer, so he was going to touch her as much as he could.

She carefully stepped over the ring of salt and slipped off her robe as she climbed into the queen-sized bed. Alex scooted to the far size to make room for him.

He climbed in beside her and laid down.

Alex curled up on his bare chest and sighed contentedly.

Tom kissed the top of her wet hair, thinking he couldn't believe how much his life had changed in just twenty-four hours.

CHAPTER
ELEVEN

Tom

Tom awoke to Alex's whimper.

They'd rolled apart in their sleep and were facing away from each other.

She struggled in the blankets. She'd somehow gotten twisted up in the sheets.

"Alex? Alex, wake up!" he said, pulling the fabric free and tugging her back to him.

She fought him, thrashing against his hold. Finally, her eyes opened. Alex blinked, looking up at him as she lay on her back, tears running down her face.

"What is it?" Tom asked, stroking her cheek.

She rolled into his arms, pressing closer, her body still trembling. "I couldn't get away," she whispered into his chest.

He pulled her even closer. "What were you dreaming about?"

"I couldn't get away," Alex sniffed. "Something was going to get me, and I couldn't get away."

Tom rubbed her bare back. "It's all right. You're safe. I won't let it get you." He kissed the top of her head and Alex quieted in his arms.

"Sorry," she cried, sitting up and wiping away her tears.

"It's just a nightmare, no big deal," he said, smiling to reassure her.

"But it didn't feel like just a nightmare. The dream was so vivid." She shivered again. "I remember the sound of something gaining on me as I ran through the trees. I could feel its breath and smell the rot of death."

Tom sat up next to her. "Why don't we go see about some coffee?" he suggested.

The sun was coming up, and the sky was lightening.

Alex nodded and crawled out of bed.

He slipped back into his room to get dressed.

Alex was in the bathroom. She was dressed in dark blue jeans and a red tank top. She'd pulled her hair up in a simple ponytail with a red ribbon tied to it.

She looked like a simple country girl instead of the fancy lady he'd always seen her as. She was still hot.

She was brushing her teeth, so Tom got his toothbrush wet and started brushing his own, standing behind her.

It was so utterly normal, so different from life on the road with his cousin. So…tempting, just like Alex.

He could see in the mirror over the top of her head, but his eyes kept going down to her backside. Especially when she bent over to rinse.

"Are you checking out my butt?" Alex teased.

Tom grinned. He rinsed his mouth. "Kinda hard not to notice the way those Wranglers hug you!"

She shook her head and grinned.

He leaned down and kissed her.

Alex stretched up on her tiptoes, but he still had to lean down to reach her.

He smacked her butt as he pulled away. "Should we go get that coffee?" he asked.

She got their new coffee maker out of the box and brewed them a pot. She scrambled a few eggs for Tom and sipped at her coffee while he ate. "So, how comfortable are you on a horse?" Alex asked.

"I can hold my own. Why do you ask?" Tom said.

"You mentioned a lake on the property. I thought we could go for a ride, maybe find where the place is. We haven't seen much of the property, besides the house and barn."

It'd been a long time since Tom had been on a horse, but it'd be helpful to get a look at the area before he a Gene went into town to take a look at the bodies of the victims.

The urgency was there, to find out if the deceased residents were in fact killed by a preternatural being. But it was early in the morning, and he doubted his cousin would be up and moving for a while. They'd have a little time to kill before they could get into the medical building and get answers.

Tom followed Alex outside and to the fenced-off area where the horses were.

"Can you help me with the saddles? They're in the back of the trailer."

An off-white trailer sat parked between the red barn and the corral. They walked around to the back, and Alex opened things up. A small door proved to be the tack room. She pulled out a saddle and handed it to Tom.

He almost dropped it at first.

Alex had been slinging it with apparent ease, and he'd misjudged the weight.

"Can you carry it over there and balance it on the fence? Then come back and get the other one? That way I can get the smaller things."

He did as requested, watching her do her thing.

She seemed to be an expert, the way she quickly brushed down both animals, then slid their saddles into place.

Tom had his doubts that she could swing the saddle up onto the big red horse, but Alex did it with ease.

When she'd finished tightening the cinches, she held out her hand for the saddlebags.

Tom handed them over, and she strapped the bags to her horse and a blanket in case they stopped later to rest.

"This is Anduril," Alex said, patting the large red horse. He was a really tall chestnut horse with a white star on his head and two white socks on his front feet.

Tom stepped over and rubbed the horse's soft nose. "Hey buddy, are you going to be nice to me today?" He let the horse smell him.

"Oh, Flame's a big baby, aren't you?" Alex said, nuzzling the horse.

"Flame? I thought you said his name was Andu-something?"

"Anduril." She said rolling the *R*. "It means 'flame of the west ' in Elvish."

"Elvish?" Tom asked, raising an eyebrow. "As in, Middle Earth?"

Alex smiled, and her cheeks lit up, as if she was embarrassed. "Yeah, I've read all the books."

He smiled. "Me too."

"Really?"

"Yeah, well, we travel a lot." Tom shrugged. "Wait, Anduril is a sword, isn't it?"

Alex smiled again. "It's Aragon's sword." She handed him the reins. "And this is Elentari," she said, showing him the smaller bay mare.

"What does that mean?" Tom asked.

"Queen of the Stars."

Tom laughed.

"That's the first time I've really heard you laugh. You should do it more often." Her smile was soft, and it made his heart trip. "Well, mount up! So we can get out of here."

He stepped up and swung himself into the saddle, waiting for Alex to adjust his stirrups.

"Are you ready?" she asked.

Tom nodded, and she vaulted up into her saddle.

*Gene

The smell of freshly brewed coffee broke through his deep sleep. It'd been years since he slept so well. He couldn't name the why, but wouldn't look a gift horse in the mouth.

Gene slipped on his jeans, so he wasn't walking around completely naked. When he stepped out and noticed Tom and Alex were already gone, he padded downstairs with bare feet and no shirt.

When he saw Jessica, his whole body reacted. She was wearing a yellow sundress with the same white apron she'd worn before, tied around the waist.

He smiled and truly felt joy. This was the first time in a very long time, that he had spent more than just a few hours with a woman. And in the last thirty-six hours, he'd done more *normal* things than he'd done in a lifetime.

He could get used to that.

But he had a job to do.

This is a job.

Gene shook that thought away. Salt and burning the ghost was the job. Not Jessica. Finding out what was leaving a trail of bodies was the job. Not playing house.

She was singing quietly to the music playing on her phone, which was tucked into the pocket of the apron, something peppy. Like a boyband. Not the vintage rock she'd played before. Her dark hair was in a long ponytail and she was barefoot, too. She smiled when she turned and saw him. "Breakfast," she said as she pointed to the small cafe table.

Gene laughed. "Pie! I get pie for breakfast?"

Jessica laughed. "Yes, and if you hurry, it should still be warm."

Gene sat at the table and took a huge bite from the piece of apple pie.

Jessica set a large cup of coffee in front of him as she sat across from him.

"How are you this morning?" he asked.

"Sore," she replied, her cheeks flushing pink with embarrassment.

Gene grinned, proud of himself. "Any sign of Tom or Alex?"

"No, they headed out on horseback a while ago."

"So we have the house to ourselves?" he wagged his eyebrows.

Jessica laughed again. "I think I need a chance to recover."

"I could massage those sore muscles for you."

"You're incorrigible. Besides, don't you have a job to do?" she reminded him.

Gene had to think for a moment. He was sure they hadn't mentioned the real reason they had agreed to stay. It wasn't the ghost, the company, or the pie. It was the unexplained deaths popping up in their small town.

"Animal?" Jessica continued.

"Oh, shit. Tuning up the van. Yeah. I'll get right on it." He shoved another large bite into his mouth.

Tom

Alex and Tom rode for a few hours, exploring the farm and the woods beyond. A trail had led through the trees, and when it opened up, there was a beautiful lake nestled in the grove. The water was a blue-green color. Ducks quacked and called to each other as they swam and floated across.

It was a breathtaking scene, not the ominous danger he was supposed to investigate. Although, on the far side of the lake was a rocky formation. The perfect place for a monster to hide. He hadn't seen any signs that a cryptid had been in the area. The news stories hadn't said where at the lake the bodies had been found, and there was no police tape visible.

They moved further back into the wooded area until they found a clearing.

Tom wasn't used to riding and his thighs were sore.

He relaxed back with his legs stretched out on the blanket, propped up on his arms.

Maybe it's not a job for us after all…

He knew better than to think like that. He just wanted to live in the moment for once.

Alex sat next to him, her legs folded in front of her.

"So how much of this is your farm?" he asked, looking around.

"Jessica's farm," she corrected in a snap.

Tom frowned at her sharp tone. Had he touched on a sensitive subject?

Her eyes moved around the scenery, taking it all in, and he followed her gaze.

"I don't know. I think the realtor sent a map of the property line, but I didn't pay close attention. She has fifty acres or something ridiculous like that."

"Wow, that's a lot of land!" he said.

"Yeah, I guess," Alex said.

"You don't sound very enthusiastic."

"It's just…" She studied his face. "I don't know… not mine." She shrugged.

"I thought you were partners in this place."

"Oh, we are. Jessica's my best friend and whatever is hers is mine and all that but…" she trailed off.

"But what?" Tom prompted.

"Well… Jessica has an online business she can totally run from here, but I had to quit my job. I thought I'd just get another one, but there's nothing around here, so now I don't know what I'm going to do."

"You could farm," Tom said, smiling.

She arched a delicate eyebrow. "I know nothing about farming."

"Okay, ranching then?" he suggested. "You know a lot about horses. Why don't you raise them?"

"I hadn't thought of that," Alex said, tilting her head to one side, as if she was truly contemplating the idea.

He sat up and leaned toward her. "Well, I think you would be great at it." He dipped toward her for a kiss.

Alex leaned into his mouth.

Tom wrapped his arms around her and kept her against him, as he laid back on the blanket.

Alex went willingly into his arms.

They kissed, each one ratcheting him hotter and hotter, until he urged her down onto the blanket on her back. He cupped her breasts over her shirt.

Alex moaned and tilted her head back.

Tom explored her neck, nipping and licking as he tasted her skin. He flipped his hair out of his way and returned to her lips, treasuring each touch.

Alex's hands slid up underneath his T-shirt, trailing her fingertips up and down his chest and back.

He shivered and moved into her strokes, wanting more.

Without warning, she grabbed the hem of his shirt and tugged it up and over his head.

When the fabric hit the blanket, something caught Tom's eye.

It was a movement in the trees.

Despite the blood and desire pounding in his temples, he stilled and then pulled back from his lover, but he hovered over her to keep her from view.

Someone—or something—was watching them.

Tom shuddered, and this time it wasn't from Alex's ministrations.

"What is it?" she asked.

"Shh... Thought I saw something."

She panted, but like him, this time it wasn't from lust. This time, it was from fear. "Should we go?" she whispered.

"Yeah, I think so." He looked down into her eyes. In the sunlight, her eyes had a green halo around the chocolate brown. He could get lost in those eyes.

Alex's moving under him brought him back to the present.

"Don't hurry," Tom said under his breath. "Move with purpose, not speed." He grabbed his discarded shirt and slipped it back on.

They packed up quickly, but quietly, and swung back into the saddle.

He let Alex take the lead as they walked the horses away from the clearing, and Tom kept an eye behind them.

Tom brought his horse up next to Alex.

She turned in the saddle when he spoke.

"Well, at least we found the lake. It doesn't look nefarious. Rather picturesque. Let's get back to the farm. Gene and I need to go to town, talk with some folks, and figure out what we're dealing with."

"Can you keep up?" Alex said.

"Only if you know where we're going."

"I hope so!" She kicked her horse to a canter and ran all the way back to the farm.

Alex stopped her horse when she could see the farmhouse.

"What is it?" Tom asked, pulling his horse up beside her.

"What do you think's out there?" She tried to hide the tremble in her voice.

"I don't know. It could just be a person," he said, offering a smile that was no doubt to make her feel better.

It didn't work. "But you don't think so," Alex said.

Tom sighed and leveled a serious gaze on her. "I won't lie to you. It doesn't do any good to lie, it would only put you in danger. But no. I don't think it's just a person."

Alex swallowed.

Tom could tell she wanted to ask what he thought it was, they both knew she didn't truly want the answer.

He was on edge, his body stiff, and his spine straight. He kept subtly glancing around them, trying his best to keep his suspicions away from Alex.

CHAPTER
TWELVE

Jessica

Jessica stood at her bedroom window, looking down at Gene, who was working on her van in the front yard.

She'd been attempting to open boxes and put things away, but her new lover was unintentionally distracting her.

His fine ass was at a perfect view, with him leaning over the insides of 'Animal', her vehicle. Every once in a while, she'd glimpse Gene wiping his forehead. Surely, he was getting hot. He'd been out there for a while with the June sun shining right on him.

Jessica shrugged and gave up. She wasn't getting any work done, she was just watching the man who'd curled her toes and rocked her world all night long. She went down to the kitchen and poured two glasses of lemonade, shutting the cupboard that refused to stay closed, on her way out.

Gene was arguing with the van about a bolt being too tight when she stepped up to him with the Southern hospitality she often saw in her favorite movies. She held a glass out to him.

His smile made her heart skip.

He reeked of bad boy, with a side of *love 'em and leave 'em*, and she needed to pin that to her brain.

They might be good together—in and out of bed, but Gene wasn't sticking around. She didn't need to get attached.

Jessica doubted he'd ever had a woman treat him well. He probably needed a good woman's touch, as much as she needed a man that actually cared about someone other than himself.

After what she'd learned about the cousins' 'jobs', it wasn't a shocker that Gene—and Tom—put others first on a daily basis.

So, if this was all she could do for him, to say thank you for the lives he'd saved over the years, then she'd be glad to. While reminding herself that she couldn't—shouldn't—get attached to him, no matter how Gene made her heart pound with a mere look, or how her body responded to his kiss and touch.

Jessica casually leaned back against the van, taking a long drink from her lemonade while she watched him work.

He grumbled to himself again about the same bolt he'd been fighting with.

She glanced under the open hood.

Gene, being the macho man he was, chuckled.

Their eyes met.

"What's wrong?" she asked.

"My hands are too big to get a good grip on this bolt," he said. He gave her an obvious once-over and smiled.

Jessica tried to ignore the sensation zinging up and down her body at Gene's perusal.

He probably thought she'd have no clue what he was talking about.

"That's the engine, and that's where you put oil when it's low," he said, pointing to various parts under the hood of her van.

She flashed a challenging smile. Then she pointed things out herself. "And that's the timing belt, that's the water pump, that's the—"

"Wait, how do you know your way around a vehicle?" Gene leaned back, crossing his arms over his broad chest. He kicked one foot out in front of the other and smirked.

He looked so damn sexy. Jessica didn't let it distract her. "Well, I've only had Animal here about a year and I haven't needed to get under the hood. But Cookie Monster, the Duster, well, I knew that one inside and out. I did all the maintenance on him."

"Seriously? I can't believe my luck. That I would stumble across a woman who can satisfy me in the bedroom, likes my type of music, makes a killer pie, and knows about cars. *If only I was the settling down type.*" He'd whispered the last, but she'd still heard him loud and clear.

Her face heated with pleasure, and she looked away before meeting his pretty green eyes again. "So what's the diagnosis, doc?" she asked, breaking the tension his whispered words caused.

"Well, he's extremely dehydrated. And dirty. Could use an oil transfusion and a power wash."

Jessica laughed that he'd played along. She hadn't expected it. "Well, oil we can do. I don't have a power washer though. I'll take Animal into town later this week and stop at the car wash. I thought I saw one when we headed to the bar." She held her hand out for the wrench he was holding.

He arched an eyebrow, his expression shouting that he didn't know why she wanted it, but he handed it to her anyway.

She handed him her glass of lemonade and found the bolt he'd been having trouble with. Jessica had to work pretty hard to get it loose, but it finally came free. She pulled it off and held it out for Gene. "Anything else?" she asked.

He smiled, slow and sexy, his green eyes darkening with desire.

Sweat bathed her forehead from her efforts, and the front of her dress was dirty from leaning into the van. Engine grime covered her hands and forearms.

"Damn, that was hot!" Gene breathed.

Jessica laughed. "I think Alex and Tom should be back soon, so I'm gonna get some sandwiches made. What do you like?"

He took a sauntering step toward her. "I can show you what I like," he said, his voice dropping seductively.

She laughed again and stepped away from him. "I meant on your sandwich."

His handsome face was crestfallen when he realized she wasn't going to let him seduce her, but he smiled anyway. "Surprise me!" he called after her.

Jessica went inside and cleaned up, then busied herself in the kitchen, preparing sandwiches for everyone. She switched her playlist from her mullet rock to her playlist called The Feels. Her favorite song on that playlist, *'My Love'* by *Razor's Edge* was playing.

The song lulled to an instrumental section and something caught her attention.

Was it outside or inside?

She paused the music, cocking her head to listen intently.

There was nothing.

She must've imagined. Jessica shook her head and started the music again. She wasn't done making lunch.

The song ended and before another began; and in the intervening quiet seconds, she swore she heard it again.

A very soft woman's voice.

Jessica paused the music again.

Waited a few heartbeats.

Nothing.

"It's likely all in my head," she spoke out loud to herself. "Alex's got me all worked up now, thinking this house is haunted." Jessica started the music back up, but this time, instead of listening to the song, she listened to everything else around her.

The ticking of the old clock above the stove, the slow drip of water in the sink, the odd settling of the house.

The intensity of her silent efforts made her temples throb, and she reminded herself to breathe. She needed to let it all go. All she could hear was the typical house noises. Yet, she'd clearly heard the words.

It wasn't coming from her phone.

"Edith. My Edith."

Jessica turned off her phone, and her skin erupted in gooseflesh. She'd listened to this playlist a million times and had never heard a woman's voice in the background.

Her hands shook as she returned to making lunch. She had a hard time spreading the mayonnaise because her fingers were far from steady.

"You okay there Jessica? You look like you saw a ghost." Gene filled the doorframe.

She hadn't heard him come in; she jumped back and threw the knife in the air, and it clattered to the old wood floors. Jessica grabbed her throat and gasped. Her heart was racing a mile a minute. "Oh, my goodness. You scared me half to death!"

Jessica told herself to breathe through her fright and shook her head. Should she tell him what she heard, or would he think she was crazy?

Gene wouldn't think she was crazy. He hunted monsters and had something called a serpent sword in his bag. If anyone would understand, it would be Gene.

She should tell him.

"Sorry, I didn't mean to scare you," he said, as he went to the sink and began scrubbing the grease from his hands.

She nodded and swallowed. "Listen, something happened—"

"Tell me." His green eyes were intense as they landed on hers, while he washed up.

Jessica told him what had happened with her music. She offered him a plate with a sandwich and some chips on it.

He took it, with a quiet thanks, encouraging her to continue as he took a seat at the little café table.

Much to her disgust, Gene asked her questions as he ate his sandwich, showing off his mouth full of food.

Alex was right. He was definitely not *the* one.

"Did the room suddenly get cold?" he asked.

"I'm sorry, what? I couldn't understand you with your mouth full of food," Jessica said, with an arched eyebrow. They'd shared other meals together, but he hadn't eaten like this before.

"Did the temperature drop?" Gene swallowed the food in his mouth.

"I don't think so. I just was standing here making sandwiches, and I heard it."

"But you saw nothing?"

Jessica shook her head.

"Could you understand what it said?" he asked, his handsome face intense again.

"She called me Edith. My great-grandmother was named Edith. She died when I was five, I think."

Gene took another bite of his sandwich, then headed upstairs without another word to her.

Jessica frowned. What the hell was going on?

Asking for help was a challenge for her, and Gene had just walked away?

She sighed and went to clean up the sandwich-making supplies.

Gene came back moments later with something in his hands that was chirping and whistling. "Well, it's picking up something, so you do have a ghost," he said.

"Uh, what do I do now?" Jessica's heart raced all over again. She believed in ghosts, but they were always somewhere else. Now that there was one in the house she was living in, she was... terrified. A chill stiffened her spine and made her limbs shake worse than earlier.

"That's easy. We just dig up the bones and salt and burn them," Gene said, as if he was talking about changing the oil in her van. He sat down to finish his sandwich.

"But I don't even know who she is," Jessica said.

"We'll do some research. But I have a pretty good idea."

It wasn't relaxing, even if it was confirmation she wasn't crazy and there truly was a ghost, but at least Gene was willing to help her. That brought her a little comfort.

CHAPTER
THIRTEEN

Gene

Gene stepped out onto the porch when his cousin and the ebony-haired woman returned, their two horses kicking up a load of dust. "Well, I wondered where you two'd run off to."

"We found the lake," Tom said, slipping out of the saddle.

"How far is it?" he asked.

"About a mile east of here."

Alex grabbed the reins out of Tom's hand and led the horses back to the corral.

"Did you see anything?" Gene asked, waiting until she was out of earshot. He met his cousin's hazel eyes.

"There's something out there," Tom said.

"Any idea what?" He folded his arms.

"No, I didn't get a good look at it. I think we should head to town and look at those bodies."

"All right, let's suit up," Gene said. He pushed off the porch wall and whirled toward the front door.

"I'm going to shower before we leave." Tom headed upstairs.

He didn't answer his cousin because Jessica had just come out of the kitchen.

"What's going on?" she asked, drying her hands on her apron.

"Tom and I have to go to town and do a little investigating."

"But you'll be back, right?" Jessica took a step closer to him.

Gene studied her pretty face. She needed reassurance. Despite the sex, he refused to assign a status to where they stood. Did he want to...?

She had a ghost problem, and needed help with her van, but they weren't going to end up together, or some shit.

As soon as the ghoul or werewolf, or some other supernatural being problem was resolved, he and his cousin would leave. Like always...

Jessica stirred feelings within him. Feelings that were about more than fucking. She made Gene feel somehow... needed.

Not just for his skill set, but as a man in general. The feelings were a distraction he couldn't afford, and he just needed to hit the road again.

He didn't have time to get bogged down with some dame. That wasn't the life. Yet...

"Gene?" Jessica brought his attention back. She tossed the hand towel over her shoulder and leaned against the door frame. "You are coming back after you go into town?"

"Unless you want us to go? We can take care of the problem away from the farm, so you can get back to your new life," he said. He needed a distraction from her tempting face and the need to kiss her.

However, something that looked like hurt darted across her eyes. Jessica visibly swallowed. "Do what you need to." She pivoted on her heel and returned to the kitchen, not waiting for an answer.

Gene sighed. He should be relieved she'd backed off instead of pushing him, but he couldn't leave her like that. Hurt, because of him. Before he could address it, he needed to change.

He whirled toward the stairs, only hesitating for one heartbeat, before shaking his head and going to his room.

They met again on the stairs, Jessica only a few steps up, a basket of laundry perched on her shapely hip. She stopped, frozen in her tracks, and gave him an obvious once-over.

He barely was able to hold the smirk in, running his hand down the front of his dark gray suit, smoothing out any remaining wrinkles. Under the jacket, he wore a white button-up shirt and a red tie.

The look on Jessica's face said it all.

However, he wanted to hear it from her.

"What?" Gene arched an eyebrow.

Jessica shook her head. "Nothing. You just look..."

"Like a monkey in a suit," he said, trying to sound serious. He schooled his expression.

"I was gonna say hot," Jessica said.

Gene flashed a devilish smile. "Really? Well, maybe when I get back, we can play a little boss and secretary."

Her cheeks lit up and an appealing red. "Does that mean you're coming back?"

"Well, yeah." He cleared his throat. "I mean, we do need to be here to get rid of your ghost."

He'd hurt her again. The crestfallen look in her beautiful eyes said it all.

Gene sucked back a sigh. He needed to fix things with Jessica before he left. However, before he could repair the new damage he'd done, Tom came out of the bathroom with a suit on as well. His hair was still damp from his shower.

"Ready?" his cousin asked.

He nodded, and they headed down the stairs.

Tom and Gene drove into the small town of Broken Bow. With barely three thousand people, aside from a post office, and a dozen churches, there wasn't much else.

The coroner's office was in the basement of the brand-new medical center. The place still had the lingering smell of fresh paint.

The off-white brick building wasn't quite a full-fledged hospital, even though it did have an emergency department. It was easy to find the morgue; they just followed the signs.

After flashing their fake CDC badges, and their winning smiles at a young woman, she took them to the coroner without question.

The room was small, with only four body lockers and one autopsy/embalming table.

"Why is the CDC interested in animal attacks?" the coroner asked. She was an older woman, probably mid-sixties. Her white lab coat covered a gray blouse that made Gene think she looked half-dead.

"We're comparing cases from different states to figure out if there may be a rabies epidemic crossing the country," he said.

"All right. Well, all the victims look like a cougar or a bear had eaten them, even though neither animal is known to attack humans in this area," she said, pulling out a drawer and showing them the last victim.

It was hard to distinguish if it was male or female because it was so torn up. A lot of bones were sticking out of the corpse.

"And where did you say they found these people?" Gene asked.

"Near Lake George."

"I'm sorry, Lake George?" Tom asked, taking down a note on a small tablet.

"Yeah, It's on the outskirts of town. It was named after a local resident, George Ferguson, after his wife killed him, then disappeared."

"You're sure it was his wife?" his cousin arched an eyebrow.

"Well, it was long before my time," the coroner said. "Back in the early 1900s, George and Judith Ferguson lived just north of town. Small town, big stories. Even though the lake is on the

Ferguson land, it has always been a popular place. Everyone knows about the Ferguson place. As the story goes, he was murdered in the summer of 1915 and left out for the animals to finish off. Not much of him was left when they found him. They got lucky with a bit of weathered skin still clinging to the gnawed-on bone of the left humerus. Ol' George had a tattoo of his wife's name. Something to show they were well off. Just enough of the tat was viable to identify. They couldn't prove Judith did it. But when she ran off a short time later, they closed the case. Blamed it on the wife."

"Interesting," Gene said, playing off disinterest, when he really had a dozen questions to ask. He needed to focus on one problem at a time. The ghost in the house wasn't causing the girls any harm. Whatever killed this person could come for Jessica and Alex. "So they never found Judith's body?"

"No. Last I heard, their granddaughter, Marge was living in their old place, but she's gone, too. People say the place is cursed. I feel sorry for whoever takes over the property."

Tom coughed. "The bodies?" He tapped on the edge of the slab, bringing everyone back to the situation at hand.

"Can you think of anything these victims had in common?" Gene asked. They didn't need to mention to the coroner that someone new *had* moved into Marge's place. "Same blood type, or were they related?"

"No. One was O positive, another A, and one AB negative. Two men and a woman."

"Were they missing any organs? Say a heart?" Tom asked.

"They were all missing some or parts of their organs, as is common in animal attacks. Mr. Jones, here, has his heart intact."

He exchanged a look with his cousin. This ruled out a werewolf. Their choice part was the heart.

Looking over the body, Gene didn't suspect a ghoul, either. The eating pattern didn't match. Every ghoul he'd encountered in all his years of hunting had gnawed on the body like some people eat corn on the cob, from one side to the other, or top to bottom.

This body had no pattern. Just torn to shreds and devoured at random.

"Thank you very much for your time," he said as they left.

Jessica

Jessica returned to her room to finish unpacking. Alex had gone to lie down for a nap after finishing up with the horses, so she didn't worry about her. She was excited to use the built-in bookcase on the left wall in her room. It was made of sturdy oak, belying its age. It was floor to ceiling, with four sections, eight shelves on each, totaling twenty-four shelves.

She quickly filled one section with her first two boxes. One box held books, but the other held knick-knacks and mementos of her life. Jessica aligned the books to allow her to place a memento in between, like a bookend.

Moving on to the third and last box she'd hauled upstairs, she ran across an old childhood diary. The cover was faux leather, stained a cherry color. The faded words *My Diary* were embossed in gold. A tiny latch that once had a key to lock the secrets of a young girl was long ago broken, the tab hanging precariously from the edge, one misstep away from ripping off.

Jessica lovingly ran her finger over the top, flooded with happy memories of a little girl living in Portland. Beautiful memories that hadn't known intense pain or grief. When her worst fear was if a certain boy liked her or not.

The desire to reminisce outweighed the need to unpack. She moved over to the squeaky bed, sat on the edge, and began to flip through the small book. This had been her third diary, starting her senior year in high school. She'd written in it almost daily. Such were the dramas of teenage life.

.   .   .

August 23rd,

Marching band tryouts were today! I've been working on my pole tossing all summer and landed the first toss perfectly! I only dropped my pole once. Angela, the stupid captain of the Color Guard, dropped her pole like fifteen times. I asked Alex if she saw, but she was too busy trying to hit the notes right on her flute while following the steps to the field design.

Jessica thumbed a few pages further.

September 28th,

Mom found out why I joined the Marching Band. She thought I wanted to show school spirit or hang out with Alex. I love my best friend, but she said something in front of Mom about if I noticed how hot Kirk looks in the new uniforms. Mom asked Alex if that was her crush, and she threw me under the bus! I'm so mad at Alex!

Jessica couldn't help but laugh at that. She'd forgiven Alex for that misstep a long time ago. She read some entries, flipped ahead, and read a few more.

October 18,

I went to Laurie's eighteenth birthday party last night. She had a fortune teller there. I had my palm read. Crazy lady said someday I'd be a business owner doing what I love.

Jessica nodded. That'd worked out to be true. She had found something she was passionate about and had turned it into a business.

• • •

I asked her about my true love. She said one day I'd meet my soulmate and we would have instant chemistry, but there would be something dark and hidden that would try to tear us apart. Well, that rules out Kirk. I already know him. I guess I don't mind. He started dating Angela last week, and who wants those sloppy seconds?

Her mind drifted from her teenaged musings.

What had ever happened to Kirk and Angela?

What could've happened if *she* had dated Kirk? Would that have prevented her from journeying down the path that eventually led her to Justin?

Justin, his dark brown eyes and matching dark hair he kept buzzed, made him a very good-looking man. He held a very dark soul.

Her eyes stung with tears. She'd loved Justin so much. He'd been kind and thoughtful when they'd started dating. He'd been her first love.

Her first everything.

Then he'd turned out to be a monster.

Jessica rubbed at her right femur, over the vine tattoo she had inked to hide the ugly scars. Justin had broken it in three places when he'd stomped the heel of his heavy boots on her leg. One of many injuries that still haunted her when the weather changed.

Glancing back at the book, she sighed. The fortune teller was right about everything and now she had no hope of finding love, because her soulmate had chosen the dark side. She chuckled. She could relate to Padme in Star Wars.

She almost closed the book, but something nagged at her to finish reading the entry.

She said I'd know him by the star he carries over his heart and his baby horse.

· · ·

Jessica gasped. She almost dropped the book.

"How did I not remember that part?" she asked the empty room. "Justin had nothing that resembled a star, but Gene..." Her hand went to her mouth.

Gene had a pentagram or hexagram, or something weird like that, tattooed on his chest that, at first glance, looked like a star.

Her heart hammered so hard that her pulse throbbed in her temples.

Gene is my soulmate?

Could that be what this meant?

She reread it twice, comparing Gene and Justin. She did have instant chemistry with Gene, but she and Justin had dated a while before anything physical happened.

With Justin, she'd often doubted what he'd told her out of instinct. With Gene, Jessica just trusted him, even after she'd found out he'd lied about his profession.

After all, she didn't truly know him, but she'd already had sex with him. It was like instant trust, too.

You will know him by the star he carries over his heart and his baby horse.

Baby horse still made no sense. Her mind flashed back to the previous morning when they'd been getting ready to leave.

"Do you like my baby?" Gene had asked her.

Jessica pulled out her phone and googled the word Mustang. Several pictures of cars appeared. So did images of beautiful horses. She paced her room, talking to herself.

"Can this be right? Could *Gene* be my soulmate? He's not planning on staying. He's just here for a hunt, then he'll leave," she said. Her limbs shook, and a sense of fright and lack of control snaked their way up her spine, making her stomach and her head spin. Her chest hurt, and it was a great deal of effort to get air down.

A panic attack?

She never had panic attacks. Now, after thinking she'd never find love, he was right here, yet completely out of reach.

Gene was a drifter.

"A good woman can make any man want to stay."

Jessica's eyes shot to the bed, where the voice had come from.

There was a ghostly white form standing there, very prim, and proper, looking like she'd just stepped out of a frontier movie.

She wanted to scream, but her voice froze in her throat. She blinked, and the woman flickered and vanished.

Had she really just seen her, or was she hallucinating?

Jessica cautiously moved back to the bed, where the woman had been standing.

It was colder here, but she sensed nothing else.

"Where's Gene with his stupid gadget when I need him?" She debated going to find Alex and get some reassurance she wasn't crazy, but when she went into the hall, Alex's door was closed.

Her best friend only closed her door if she was resting or wanted to be alone and since she'd been on a long ride with Tom, Jessica figured she was just tired.

She took a deep breath and headed downstairs, grabbing a hard cider from the fridge. Maybe she just needed some fresh air to clear her head.

Jessica had always had an overactive imagination. Perhaps it was just getting the better of her. Besides, she already knew the supposed ghost situation spooked Alex.

She didn't want to confirm her suspicions. She took her drink out onto the front porch and sat down on the steps.

CHAPTER
FOURTEEN

Gene and his cousin sat in the parking lot of the small medical building, going over ideas. He glanced at the computer resting precariously on Tom's knees.

It was amazing the things they always found on the internet because his cousin always seemed to know where to look. If the cops ever got their hands on the laptop, they'd be in prison for life, blamed for all the murders and attacks they looked into, simply because of all the research they did.

"I'm still not sure," Tom sighed. "There're too many factors that don't match up for it to be a Wendigo."

"I get it. But it's the only thing that makes logical sense."

"How is this logical, Gene? I mean, I know I've only been doing this a few years, but everything points to them only being active in the winter months. It's June. And I don't think they have ever traveled this far south before. Part of Minnesota, yes. But Nebraska? I don't think so." He shook his head, scattering his too-long locks.

"You do your thing, and look it up, I'm gonna find us lunch."

Gene pulled the car out of the parking lot and hit the road, wheels screeching on the asphalt.

"Hey, stop at that little grocery store we saw on the way in. The girls have an old grill in the barn. We could cook up something at their place."

"Fine, but we need to stop for a beer while you look shit up," he said.

They sat at the booth at the dive bar where they'd met the girls. The place wasn't any better looking in the daytime than it had been at night.

The floors were still as dirty and sticky as before. Neon lights advertising various beers didn't seem to shine as brightly, though. However, the burgers were heaven.

Gene had a mouthful of his double meat, double cheese, extra bacon, no veggies burger, and mustard smearing the corner of his lips.

His cousin was mad taping at the keys on his laptop, ignoring the impossible burger in front of him. "Well, this might help. It says here that in 1892 there were eighteen different treaties for the Nebraska/Dakota and Minnesota tribes. Settlers were moving into the area and stripping it of its resources, pushing the tribes out of their known homes. Tribes were moved to territories they weren't familiar with, and many died from starvation. In the summer of 1899, over 500 tribe members had perished."

"So, it is possible?" Gene asked.

"I think so. Here's another article from the *Lincoln Evening Call*, from April 1912. A man claims the chief of a nearby tribe owes him money for his dog killing the farmer's chickens. But the chief refuses to pay, saying if his people aren't left alone, he will call upon the Wendigo to end the feud. With the man's death."

He dropped his half-eaten burger on the plate. "Hold on... A chief can control a Wendigo? I've never heard that before."

"I think it was just a threat. The article goes on to say the tribe moved north, getting closer to South Dakota and the farmer was at ease." Tom finally picked up his 'fake' burger and took a bite.

"I don't know how you can eat the shit," Gene teased.

"Could say the same thing about your meal."

"Bullshit. Bacon is its own food group. Anyway, I think our best strategy is to look for a possible nest near the lake. Usually, Wendigos store their meals—"

"Yeah, but that's meant to last them all winter, during times of starvation."

"But if he's feasting on flesh during the summer," Gene jumped back in, "he's not worried about dragging the corpse away to save for later, he's crunching and munching whenever he wants."

"He'd still have a place to nest. Let's get back to the farm. I can finish my research there."

"You just want to get back to Alex. I can see it in your beady eyes," Gene teased.

"Like you don't want to go back, too." Tom winked, and his smile was a bit too knowing.

He threw his napkin at his cousin, not agreeing, yet saying no either.

Gene grinned when he pulled in and saw Jessica sitting on the porch, waiting for him. He chastised himself for being so pleased to see her. This couldn't last long.

Sure, it was nice to dream about being a normal guy. He'd never get to have that.

A normal life.

Very soon, he'd have to hit the road with Tom, like always.

Stepping out of his car, Tom on his heels, the thoughts of the Wendigo slipped away.

There was only her.

This was bad, and he was in trouble, but Gene ignored those thoughts too.

Jessica patted the steps beside her and offered him a sip of her spiked cider.

Gene let his cousin slip past them to head inside before he sat down.

She seemed on edge, and it bothered him. He took a moment to truly see her, notice the agitated tap of her right foot, or the fact the bottle of cider no longer had a label on it.

"What's going on?" he asked.

"I saw her," Jessica said.

"Who?"

"The ghost. She appeared in my bedroom and gave me some advice, then vanished."

"She gave you advice?" Gene smirked and arched an eyebrow.

"Yes."

"What did she say?"

"Well..." Jessica averted her pretty eyes as the blush spread over her high cheekbones like she had something she couldn't speak out loud. She shook her head hard. "That's not really the point. The point is, I saw her and she's old."

"Well, honey, ghosts usually are," Gene said, chuckling. "And dead."

She puffed up a little and met his gaze as if he'd pissed her off. "No, I mean she was dressed like Little House on The Prairie."

He cocked his head to one side. This fell in line with what the coroner said. "Well, it's definitely the same ghost your aunt was seeing. Judith Ferguson."

"My great-great-grandmother? So what do I do if I see her again?" Jessica asked, as if she was trying to remain calm, but he didn't miss the frantic undertones.

"Ask her where her bones are," Gene said.

"You're not even taking this seriously," she accused, rushing to her feet, then stormed into the house.

He grumbled to himself about women and hormones as he rose to follow her inside. He *was* taking the ghost seriously. He'd just told her what she needed to do, after all.

• • •

"So get this," Tom said to Gene, as he and Jessica came into the dining room. He'd set up his computer at the table to work. "I've been looking up information on George and Judith Ferguson. Legend has it that Judith Ferguson had always been a little… different. Talking to people who weren't there, that kind of thing. Then one day, George doesn't come back from fishing. They found his body near the lake, and wild animals had torn him up. The authorities thought Judith killed him and left him there because she disappeared around the same time and no one ever saw her again."

"No clue to what happened to her?" Gene asked.

"No one knows. Rumors abound that she still haunts the shores of Lake George. There are people who claim they've seen her, but of course, nothing concrete. I'm wondering, though, could the Wendigo have killed George?"

Jessica gasped.

"What?" Gene asked, not getting to answer his cousin.

She pointed at the computer screen. "That's her! That's who I saw in my bedroom."

The news story showed a black and white photo of a man and woman, in their early forties, dated 1915. It showed them in front of the house Jessica now owned. The woman was holding a pie dish and they were both smiling, the man's hand on her lower back. Something very uncommon at that time.

"That's who you saw?" Gene asked, frowning.

"The ghost in my room! That's her!"

"It looks like Granny stuck around," he said.

"So… what are we talking about? A vengeful spirit or what?" Tom asked.

"Vengeful?" Jessica asked.

"Yeah, that's the kind that likes to hurt people," Gene said, "I'm not sure that's what she is, though."

"Well, if it is Judith, we should take precautions. It sounds like she was insane during her life, so there's a good chance she still is," Tom said.

"Does that mean she might hurt one of us?" Jessica asked.

"Sometimes."

Her hand fluttered to her throat. "Alex! What if she's not napping? She's been up there for so long." She took off in a hurry, bolting for the stairs.

Gene and Tom exchanged a look, then followed.

*Alex

Alex almost jumped out of her skin when Jessica burst through her bedroom door. She'd just woken up and was a little shaky from having another dream that she was being chased.

She was trying to remember what'd happened, but the details were quickly fading. This time, she'd been trying to save her true love, but something had gone horribly wrong and she'd ended up in complete darkness.

Alex couldn't find her way through the darkness and panicked. She tried to hold back her tears, but it was no use.

Tom and Gene were on her best friend's heels and were in the doorway just as Jessica slid through the circle of salt and landed on the bed.

She hugged her tightly.

Alex didn't hesitate to hug her back, but why was Jessica so shaken? She couldn't know about the dream.

"Tom thinks my great-great-grandmother's ghost is still here and possibly crazy. I hadn't seen you in hours and was worried she got to you," Jessica babbled out.

Alex just shook her head. "I don't think so. It doesn't feel crazy here, just scary," she said, remembering her experience with the so-called ghost.

"I hate to disagree," Tom said, leaning against the door frame.

"But if a person is violent in life, they are the same way in death. Same thing with crazy, only without reality to hold them in check, they become worse."

Alex stiffened at the pretentious tone in his voice. She frowned.

"We need to take precautions just in case," Tom said. "Salt around the beds is a good starting point."

"Salt?" Jessica asked, glancing at the broken circle on Alex's floor. "What does that do?"

"Ghosts can't cross the salt, so as long as you're in the circle and the circle isn't broken, you should be safe," Tom said. "I'll see if I can dig up anything else on Judith."

"Well, I think we could all use a distraction tonight," Gene said with a smile.

Alex didn't miss how her bestie blushed.

He clapped. "You two are in for a treat. Tom saw an old grill out in the barn. While we were in town, we picked up stuff so I could barbecue some ribs. Jessica, since my mountain of a cousin is going to do research, can you help me bring it out?"

Jessica glanced at her.

"I'll be okay." Alex smiled.

Jessica hugged her one more time and hurried out with Gene.

Tom sat on the bed next to Alex. "There is more to your fear right now, than just a simple ghost. Tell me, what's truly bothering you."

Alex wiped at the tears that still lingered on her cheeks. "It's these dreams I've been having. I don't get nightmares often, but when I do, they never feel like this. It's so real."

"Can you remember anything about them? Dreams can sometimes hold truths we aren't ready to accept in our wakened state."

Alex explained what little she could pull back to memory. She'd never been good at remembering her dreams, not like her bestie could.

"In the darkness, I saw a bluish light. It was almost purple. It was so far away. I didn't want to be in the darkness but the light gave off an evil vibe. I wish I could explain it better!"

Tom wrapped his strong arms around her and held her together. Alex wasn't sure what she'd do if the nightmares continued after they left.

Don't think about that…

CHAPTER
FIFTEEN

*Jessica

Jessica felt the cold rush over her skin as soon as she and Gene entered the barn.

He was excited to get the grill, telling her he hadn't had the pleasure of barbecuing in far too long. He had to have felt the temperature change too, but he said nothing.

She got more and more anxious as they walked toward the back of the barn. There were paddocks in the front half on both sides and plenty of storage space in the back.

As they got closer to the grill, the air was harder to breathe. Jessica's heart pounded quick and hard, yet Gene kept going on and on about different types of meat he could be cooking.

How does he not feel the tension in the air?

They got to the very back, and there were lots of freestanding wooden shelves, some of them had paint cans on them, old tools, and such. Just past that, in the corner, was a grill.

Jessica couldn't understand how Tom could have possibly seen the grill. She never would've even noticed it was there.

Maybe it was a guy thing.

She didn't know, and she didn't care. She just wanted to get out of the barn as fast as possible. When she grabbed one side of the grill to lift with Gene, the barn felt freezing cold.

Jessica could see Gene's breath in front of him, but he still didn't seem to notice it.

There was a flicker of something by one of the wooden shelves. It didn't last long enough for her to get a good look. However, as it flickered away, she could swear the name *Edith* was whispered in the wind.

The grill was big and heavy, but it wasn't a big deal. She walked in her high heels faster than Gene could back up in his dress shoes.

She kept giving him crap about needing to go faster, and he complained she needed to quit pushing so hard. Jessica's lungs lightened, and the air seemed easier to breathe the moment they stepped over the threshold.

"You want to explain to me what happened back there?" she asked with genuine curiosity, trying to hide the slight hint of fear in her voice.

"Well, if you weren't in such a big hurry to get out of there, I wouldn't have almost tripped walking backward."

"Dammit Gene, you know that's not what I'm talking about!" Jessica shouted. It was a good thing she was still carrying the grill because she wanted to smack him. She was completely freaked out.

Why isn't he taking this seriously?

Tom seemed to be. That was why he wanted to put salt around everybody's bed and do more research.

What the hell is Gene's problem?

He set down his end of the grill, even before they had reached the porch.

Jessica set her side down and put her hands on her hips.

"I don't know what you're talking about. The only problem we had back there was you pushing me. Where were you going in such a hurry, anyway?"

"I'm talking about the flicker of a ghost and the cold air and the name Edith. How did you miss that? I even saw the cold affect your breath!"

Gene frowned and met her eyes. "I'm a hunter. I have been a hunter since I was nine years old. I know when a ghost is present, and I felt nothing. Don't take this wrong, honey, but you may be as crazy as your great-great-grandmother. There was no ghost in there. Just a dirty old barn."

Shock rolled over Jessica and she gaped. What'd he just say?

He'd…called her crazy.

She wasn't usually violent, but anger and fear boiled her blood and lifted her hand. She slapped his handsome face and whirled away without a word.

Jessica stomped up the porch steps and went into the house.

Damn Gene and what she was feeling for him.

He couldn't be her soulmate.

Frustrated, she stormed up the front stairs and into the house. Her hands and dress were dirty from bumping against the barbeque grill as she carried it. A sly grin spread across her face when she decided what to change into.

She put on a very fitted stretch red pencil skirt and a white blouse that dipped rather low. If Gene was gonna be like that, she was going to make him pay for it.

Checking from the window that the guys were still outside, she came back downstairs and into the kitchen, where Alex had music playing.

Jessica grabbed two hard ciders from the fridge and opened them before handing one to Alex. She leaned against the kitchen counter and chugged down half of her bottle of hard cider.

"You okay?" Alex asked.

"Maybe he's right, maybe I am crazy. He is a hunter, and he should've seen whatever I thought I saw," she said, taking another long pull from the bottle.

"He should have, but that doesn't mean he did," her bestie said.

"What d'you mean?"

"I mean, I think your great-great-grandmother is trying to communicate with us. I was having the craziest dream, and I swear I can feel her all around us." Alex looked at her bottle and slowly began peeling the label off with nervous fingers.

Jessica straightened. "Well, whether or not I actually saw her, Gene was still a jerk."

"Is that why you changed?" her friend teased.

She smoothed her skirt, even though it wasn't really necessary. "I just don't want him to forget what he's missing."

Alex laughed. "I'm pretty sure you've just met your match in Gene. You're used to being able to sweet talk your way into anything, but he isn't the type to fall for your feminine charms."

"Well, even if he's a jerk, I still need to be a decent hostess, I suppose. Can you get me two beers out of the fridge?" Jessica asked, ignoring her best friend's statement. She didn't want to admit anything about Gene. She had far from forgiven him for calling her crazy.

Alex grabbed two beers and popped the tops off before handing them over.

Jessica took them and headed for the porch, ignoring her friend's soft laugh.

*Gene

Gene touched his face as he watched Jessica walk in the house. She'd slapped him so hard there had to be a handprint on his cheek.

He flexed his jaw and could swear he felt each one of her fingerprints with individual throbs. Her temper amused and aroused him, as did the extra saunter in her hips as she walked up the stairs, stomping her heeled feet as she went. She even had the audacity to slam the door behind her.

. . .

"Dude, what the hell did you do to Jessica? She looked pretty pissed off," Tom said, as he jogged down the front porch steps.

Gene looked up from inspecting the grill. "She was saying there were ghost signs when there wasn't anything there. I called her out on it. At first, I thought she was just spooking herself out. But then it sounded like she googled the signs of a ghost and started listing them off."

Tom stepped up to the other side of the grill and helped him continue to carry it up to the wrap-around porch. "Seriously? How many ghosts have we seen that other people can't? What did she experience?"

"She said it was cold, and she saw my breath. I felt nothing," Gene argued. "I made the mistake of calling her crazy, like her family."

Tom rolled his eyes. "You're falling for her, and you're pushing her away because you're scared." His cousin kept his voice even, conversational.

"What the hell are you talking about? Dude, crazy runs in her family. You think I want to get tangled up in that?" Gene replied. Even he could hear the defensiveness in his own voice. He stood there a moment, contemplating what really happened.

It was possible that Jessica would have a connection to the ghost, assuming it was her great-great-whatever. Family.

It wasn't the first time they'd been in a situation where the ghost was keeping its presence isolated to a single person.

Gene walked back to the barn, paying closer attention to his surroundings. He moved to the back, where the grill had been.

No cold spots. No weird sounds.

People were known for spooking themselves into seeing things that weren't there. In his line of work, it was a daily occurrence. Knowing there was a ghost, didn't help the situation. Jessica wasn't freaking herself out. There was a legitimate reason for her to be scared.

He stood there in the silence of the barn, rethinking his choice of words.

He'd been harsh with Jessica. He wasn't even sure why.

Was he mentally pushing her away?

He knew he owed her an apology.

He owed her more than just words.

Tom

Tom retrieved the meat from the kitchen, stopping to kiss Alex before he went back outside. Gene was getting the grill started, so he set the plate of raw meat on the side tray of the barbeque and returned to the porch, where he'd left his laptop. Tom took up residency in an old wooden rocking chair with his computer on his lap.

Tempting aromas were wafting from the grill by the time Jessica opened the front door.

Tom looked at her and smirked.

Gene had met his match.

There was no way Jessica was going to back down from the big, bad hunter.

He glanced over to see Gene focusing down on the grill to avoid looking at her.

She handed him to him, then walked over to Gene and set the other beer on the shelf attached to the grill.

"So, did you find anything when you went on your ride?" she asked Tom, not looking Gene's way.

"Yeah. There's definitely something out there," he replied.

"Any idea what?"

He looked over at Gene, but his cousin was still focused only on the grill.

"We think it's a Wendigo."

"You mentioned that word before. What's a Wendigo?" she asked.

"It's a human that, for one reason or another, has turned to cannibalism," Gene said, flipping the meat.

"The Algonquian tribes believed that if you eat human flesh, it gives you supernatural powers," Tom said.

"Was the whole tribe cannibals?" Jessica asked.

"No. Although you gain speed and agility, you also get an unquenchable hunger. They used the legend of the Wendigo to discourage greed and gluttony," Tom explained.

"Can you kill it?" Her voice shook.

"Yeah, you can kill a Wendigo with fire," Gene said, busying his hands by pulling the ribs off the grill.

"Fire? So you go after it with torches?" Jessica asked. "Like an old-fashioned mob with torches and pitchforks going after this thing?"

"Actually, we've found that flare guns work pretty well," Tom said, holding the front door open for Gene, carrying the plate of ribs.

Tom saw him do a double take when he finally caught sight of Jessica in her painted-on red skirt that stopped a few inches above her knees and a tight white blouse that showed just the right amount of cleavage.

A broad grin spread over Gene's face.

Tom changed his focus when he saw Alex setting potato salad on the table.

She looked so natural here that he could imagine coming home to her after a hunt, and letting her wipe away the bad memories with her soft touch.

They all sat in the same seats as they had the night before and began filling their plates.

"How do you hunt it?" Jessica asked, getting the conversation back on the monster.

"Hunt what?" Alex asked., her posture tensing.

"They think there's a Wendigo down by the lake," she said.

"A Wendigo?" Alex's brown eyes went wide.

"Yeah, it's a—" Jessica said.

"I know what a Wendigo is. I just didn't know they were real," Alex said.

"It's all right. Gene and I will take care of it," Tom said, putting a comforting hand on Alex's thigh.

"So how do you hunt it?" Jessica asked again, this time directed at Gene.

He seemed to be lost in thought, so she asked again. "Gene, how do you hunt it?"

"Huh? Oh, um. We have to find its lair," he stumbled out, catching up in the conversation.

Tom could guess by the guilty look on Gene's face exactly where his thoughts had drifted. He had to admit that he would find it hard to concentrate if Alex had been dressed like that.

"Where might that be?" she asked. She seemed caught between fascination and revulsion.

"It's usually in a cave. They prefer dark places with enough space to store their victims," Tom said before he could.

"Store their victims?" Alex repeated. "That's disgusting."

"Wendigos are used to going long periods of time with no food. When they get the chance, they hide their victims, usually alive, for as long as possible," Gene said.

"So there may be people alive out there that are trapped?" Alex asked, sitting up straighter.

"From what I can tell through my searching, ten other people have gone missing in the last month." Tom sighed. "Not to mention the missing people from the last one hundred years. Most were written off as people who left to start a new life. But I think the Wendigo has been here a long time, feasting as he likes."

"Hold up! *Ten*! We need to go help them!" Alex said, rising from her chair.

Tom applied a little pressure on her leg, tugging her back into her seat.

"Easy there, tiger," Gene said, smirking. "These things aren't easy to hunt."

Tom smiled. He admired her newfound bravery. He knew how scared she was of the benign ghost. He also knew how dangerous the Wendigo was. But she seemed more concerned for the victims, then her own safety.

"But those people are out there, and they're scared. That thing could kill them," Alex pleaded.

"Unfortunately, more than likely it already has," Tom said. "The most recent three people listed as missing are the ones that just turned up dead by the lake."

"But what if it hasn't?" Jessica asked. "We need to get out there and find them."

"*We?*" Gene arched an eyebrow.

"Yes, we. You can't possibly think that Alex and I are going to sit here and wait while you two go off to find this thing," Jessica said.

The guys exchanged a look. They both knew there was no way they could let the girls tag along. That was a good way to get someone killed.

"We can't hunt it until tomorrow anyway," Tom said, trying to diffuse the situation. "We need the daylight on our side."

"Is it nocturnal?" Alex asked.

"No, it is equally good at hunting during the day as it is at night, but at least in the daylight *we* can see it better," Tom said.

"What do we do until then?" she asked.

"Tom and I have a few things to get together from the car, then we wait till morning," Gene said.

CHAPTER
SIXTEEN

Jessica was in the living room hooking up the TV when the guys came back in the house, their duffle bags clinking with metal on metal sounds. She was bent over with her head behind the unit, plugging all the wires where they needed to be.

She felt, more than heard Gene behind her, and she also didn't miss the sound of retreating boots, which was probably Tom leaving them alone.

Jessica was aware that her skirt was short, and she was bent over pretty far. She didn't want him to watch her ass. She needed to hurry.

Jessica banged her head as she tried to extract herself from behind the TV. "Ow!" she exclaimed.

"Are you all right?" Gene asked, stepping closer.

She frowned. Still wanted to be mad at him. "Yeah," she replied, rubbing her head, wincing.

"Better let me look at that," he said, taking her hand and leading her to the couch.

Jessica followed, sitting down on the edge. She sighed because she had to admit she was so drawn to him. She didn't like it, but it didn't make it less true.

Damn him.

Gene slid his fingers into her hair to see if there was a bump. "I think you'll survive," he concluded, pulling his fingers away.

She wanted to close her eyes and lean into his touch, but he was gone too soon. Jessica smirked, and couldn't help it. "Thanks, doc," she teased.

They smiled awkwardly at each other for a moment.

She swallowed and fought the urge to say everything she was feeling for him that didn't make sense. She managed not to look away, even though she wanted to.

"Were you able to get it all hooked up?" Gene asked, looking at the flat screen.

"I think so. We won't have internet until I can get them out to set it up, but we could watch a DVD," Jessica said.

Gene smiled. "What do you have in mind?"

She shrugged. "There's a box of DVDs on the floor over there, if you want to pick one."

He sat on the floor pulling out movies. He held up the second *Hobbit* movie. "Does this have Rudy in it?" he asked.

She arched an eyebrow. "Who?"

"You know, the Hobbit that is Rudy? The football kid," said.

"Oh! You mean Sean Astin. He is Samwise in the *Lord of the Rings*. And no. He's only in the *Lord of the Rings* movies," Jessica said, trying not to laugh. "I think I have them in there, but they are almost three hours long, each."

He looked over his shoulder at her and shook his head.

After digging a little longer, Gene finally held up his movie choice with a smile.

Jessica giggled.

He got up off the floor and put it into the DVD player.

Without a word, she popped off the couch and headed to the kitchen.

Gene

•   •   •

The scent of popcorn tickled his nose.

A few minutes later, Jessica came back. She had a bowl full of popcorn in the crook of her left arm, with a beer in that hand. A cloth bag was looped over her right arm with a hard cider in that hand.

"I don't remember picking up popcorn at the store. How did I miss that?"

"You didn't. We already had it with us." She smiled.

"What? You just moved in, and you have popcorn?"

She handed him his beer and stepped over to the couch. "Of course we have popcorn. That's a must-have for anybody. It travels easily and most hotels have microwaves," she said. "But what's most important on movie night is in this here bag." She shook her arm up and down.

Gene took her drink from her so she could set down everything else.

She put the cloth bag down at her feet and started pulling out snacks. A bag of Reese's Pieces, M&M's, and chocolate chip cookies.

As she reached into the bag again, he touched her arm softly.

"Oh please, please tell me you've got licorice in there," he begged.

Jessica slowly pulled out an almost full bag of black Twizzlers.

He kissed her full on the lips and snatched the bag of Twizzlers from her hands. "God, I love you!" It slipped out, and she got very still.

Gene swallowed and needed to play it off, fast. He hadn't meant that…in the traditional sense. Had he?

Before either of them said something—anything. Or he did something stupid, he shoved a fistful of the black candy into his mouth, flashed a black-toothed grin, and hit play on the remote.

•   •   •

**Alex*

Alex was in her room, standing at the window, watching the sunset. She had her arms wrapped around herself, and although she heard him enter, she didn't turn when Tom came into the room.

"Alex?" he whispered.

She didn't move.

He closed the distance to her and wrapped his arms around her. "You all right?" He rested his chin on her head. She was trembling, and he held her tighter. "Don't worry. Gene and I will take care of it. You don't have to be afraid," he said.

"I'm not worried about me," she sniffed.

He turned her around and looked into her eyes.

"What if something happens to you?" she cried.

Tom smiled. "Nothing's going to happen to me. We've been hunting together for a while. Gene's been doing it almost his whole life."

"But this is different. This is a Wendigo," Alex said, feeling like it was the most horrible thing on the planet.

"A wendigo is hardly the worst thing Gene and I have faced. I've been possessed by a demon, tortured, and fought almost every monster known. We've got this." He ran his fingers through her hair. "This isn't the first Wendigo we've hunted," Tom said.

"I just have a bad feeling about this," Alex said.

"I promise we'll be careful." He pulled her closer. "Gene and I always watch each other's back."

She wrapped her arms around him.

Tom was so tall that her head rested on his sternum.

It was perfect.

"We should try to get some sleep," he said.

Alex pulled back and looked at him. "I need to clean up first. I still smell like a horse."

"Okay," he smiled.

"How about a bath?" she asked, flashing him a smile.

"You mean you want me to..."

She nodded and reached for her towel and a few candles from her bedroom, before heading to the bathroom with her goodies.

Tom had run to get his towel from his room while she started the bath.

She found her relaxing bath salts. They would help ease Tom's aching muscles.

He'd said nothing, but she knew from experience that people who weren't used to riding got very sore the first time back in the saddle.

Alex lit the candles and switched off the overhead light.

The pipes groaned as she started the water.

Tom came in and closed the bathroom door.

Alex sat on the edge of the tub, running her hand under the water. She smiled up at him.

"You sure I'm going to fit in there with you?" he asked.

"Only one way to find out," she said, going to him. Alex grabbed the bottom of his shirt and pulled it up.

He bent over so she could complete her task.

She ran her fingertips gently over his tattoo. She looked up into his hazel eyes, and he leaned down to kiss her.

Tom slid his hands under her T-shirt.

Alex raised her arms above her head so he could pull it off. She wore a simple white cotton bra with a small pink bow in the center.

He ran his fingers under the straps and slipped one from her shoulder. Tom placed a soft kiss where the strap had been, before he unfastened the back.

She reached for his jeans and pulled open the button fly. She slid his pants and boxer briefs off together, holding them while he stepped out of them.

Her hands slid along the outside of his long legs as she stood back up.

She unbuttoned and unzipped her own pants before looking back up at him.

Tom slipped his hands inside the back of her jeans and gripped her butt. He pushed her jeans and cotton panties off.

Alex stepped out of them and took his hand, leading him to the tub.

Tom sank into the warm, fragrant water while she turned off the faucet. He spread his knees apart, inviting her in.

She slipped in between his legs and rested back against his chest. She sighed comfortably while his finger glided over her body.

They sat there for a while in silence, just enjoying the peaceful environment.

Tom sighed contentedly, running his wet fingers through her hair.

"Are you worried about tomorrow?" Alex asked.

"Not really," he said.

"What if something goes wrong, though?"

"Oh, something always goes wrong."

"What?" She twisted to face him, water splashing over the edge of the tub.

"It's okay. Gene and I always adapt," he said reassuringly.

"But that thing could kill you," Alex said, frowning and trying to ignore how her heart cantered. She didn't know him, not really, but she was already very attached to this tall hunter.

"It could, but it won't," Tom said. "We've faced much worse."

Alex's vision blurred, and hot tears streaked down her cheeks. She bit the inside of her mouth, but she couldn't stop the tears.

Tom pulled her to him, and she rested her cheek against his chest.

"I plan to be back tomorrow night to see if we can figure out why your ghost is hanging around," he said.

She looked up into his eyes. "You promise?"

He smiled and pulled her into a kiss.

CHAPTER
SEVENTEEN

Jessica

Jessica was thrilled that Gene had chosen one of her favorite movies, *Dante's Peak*. It was a natural disaster movie about a volcano erupting in a small mountain town, much like Mount St. Helens in Washington. One of Jessica's favorite actresses was in it; Linda Hamilton. It made her warm all over that he'd chosen that movie. A pleasant surprise.

About halfway through the movie, he leaned forward, putting his elbows on his knees, and made an off-color comment. "She used to be one hot mama. In *Terminator Two*, hoo! Was she bangable! What happened!"

"What?" Jessica bristled, sitting forward on the couch.

"Well, you know, she packed on a few pounds and got a shit ton of wrinkles," Gene said.

She frowned and threw him a glare. "So, a girl with a few extra pounds is just fat and not attractive anymore? Nice, Gene." Jessica moved the bowl of popcorn and the M&M's she'd been enjoying on the coffee table and shot to her feet. She needed to get away from him, before she did something stupid, like give into the urge to throttle him, and headed out of the room.

The words hurt so much.

It reminded her of Justin.

Jessica made it to the kitchen before her eyes burned with the tears she refused to shed. She only cried when she was furious.

Gene came up behind her, his boots announcing his presence. "What was that about? It's not like I called you fat," he said, sounding curious, or surprised.

She couldn't look at him. If she turned around, she'd really start crying. She didn't want him to see that. "I was like that, though. Slender and fit. After Justin broke me, I thought I'd never have love again. I'd never have a reason to look good again. So, I packed on the pounds. It didn't matter if no one wanted me to have a few extra pounds. I'd lost my soulmate."

He moved closer, touching her shoulder.

"I changed for me. I took control of my life. But I'll always have a few extra pounds," she whispered.

Gene tried to turn Jessica around, but she wouldn't budge. So, he slid around to face her.

Hot tears streaked down her cheeks.

"I'll take those few extra pounds," he whispered, moving even closer. He slid his arms around her, cupping her butt. "You've got it in all the right places. I think you're sexy, as hell."

He was trying to be sweet, but it made her feel cheap. She gently pushed him away.

"You can finish the movie if you want to. I'm not feeling so good now; I'm just going to head to bed." She rubbed her temples. Jessica could feel a headache coming on.

She didn't wait for an answer, she just headed up the stairs.

Gene

. . .

Gene returned to the living room and cleaned up. His mind was running a million miles an hour. He hadn't meant to hurt her feelings. Again.

Damn.

Why are women so sensitive?

He rarely spent more than a few hours around a woman. He couldn't remember the last time he'd spent *days* with one. This was all new territory to him. And he knew he was fucking it up. Royally.

The movie was still playing, although he wasn't paying attention. He was trying to figure out how to make things right with Jessica. He didn't think she was fat. She was hot.

"*Go to her*," the disembodied whisper swirled around him.

Gene looked around but didn't see anyone. He shook his head.

The girls talking about ghosts had him…hearing things? He didn't sense—or see—a ghost. He shut off the TV and embraced the silence. Nothing. He took the popcorn and snack bag to the kitchen and swore he heard it again.

"*Go to her.*"

He spun around the room, his skin crawling with agitation. He'd never been around a ghost he couldn't sense. "Show yourself!" Gene looked around, still feeling nothing, seeing nothing. "I know you're there!"

Still nothing.

This was a waste of his time.

He was ready to storm the castle and win back his princess, or slay the dragon, he wasn't sure which waited upstairs for him. Before he could move, the temperature dropped drastically.

His breath came out in steaming puffs.

A cupboard on the right side of the kitchen opened so slightly.

His eyes shot to it.

That was it.

Gene went over to it. There was a large bottle of ibuprofen on the second shelf. "Helpful ghost?" he muttered to himself as he took the bottle. He grabbed Jessica's cider and headed upstairs.

. . .

Jessica

Jessica sat on the edge of her bed, her elbows on her knees and her face in her hands. Why was she even worried about body image?

At this point in her life, if someone didn't like her, she was fine with it. They didn't need to look at her.

So why had what Gene said, which wasn't even geared toward her, made her so upset?

The door creaked and she looked up.

Gene stood in the open doorway, a sheepish grin on his face, and rather than saying anything, he gently shook the bottle of ibuprofen he brought with him.

"How did you know?" she asked.

"A little birdie told me. More like a ghost, but you didn't hear me say that." He came into the room, offering her the bottle and her warm hard cider.

"I'm sorry I was being such a guy," Gene said, his best form of an apology. He shrugged and stuffed his hands in his pockets. His handsome face was chagrinned, but his smirk was still hot.

"I'm sorry for being such a girl. I never cry. Except for when I'm pissed off." Jessica shrugged, too.

Gene laughed. "Remind me to never piss you off, then."

"It's a little late for that," she whispered.

He gently took the meds back, popped off the lid, and dished out two pills.

"Can you make it four, please?"

"Four! That's a lot," he said.

"It's really not. They gave me 800 milligrams after Justin beat me so bad, and nothing less than 800 seems to put a dent in my pain."

Gene stared, and his brow rippled, as if he was surprised, but instantly angry. "Who is this Justin guy? You've mentioned him before."

After what Justin had done to her, Jessica swore she'd never mention him again. She hadn't, until Gene had come into her life. Nerves swirled in her tummy, making her heart skip, but she was compelled to tell him everything—even the little details.

"I started getting suspicious about his work, and later found out he wasn't just an antique dealer. He sold body parts on the black market, women from overseas into human trafficking, and many other crazy things that, at the time, I didn't understand." She took a deep breath. "When I confronted him about it, especially the human trafficking, he threatened to sell me to one of his contacts. When I tried to call the police, he beat me within an inch of my life. He broke so many bones, I felt it made me look like a completely different person. There were days I'd wished he'd killed me, because the pain was so unbearable. Not just physically, but emotionally, too."

As she told her story, she didn't miss Gene's fists clenching and unclenching. There was even a moment when his jaw flexed, like he was clenching his teeth.

"Where is this guy now?" he asked, trying to hold back obvious anger. His broad shoulders hunched and he wore a nasty scowl.

"Well, you see, Karma is a bitch. Six months ago, he died in a car accident."

"He's lucky, because if I'd gotten my hands on him..." Gene didn't finish, but he didn't have to.

She knew what he meant. It warmed her heart a bit to know he cared—even if he hadn't said so. "I just can't believe I let a stupid fortuneteller get to me like that. She was most likely just some scam artist," Jessica said, more to herself than anything.

"Some are, but I've met a few that weren't."

"Really?" Jessica asked, meeting his eyes.

He had his head cocked to one side. Gene sat on the bed next to her. "Sure. The real ones usually tell you stuff you don't want to hear, though."

"Like how my soulmate and I would be torn apart by something dark?" she asked.

He chuckled. "Yeah, that sounds about right."

"Doesn't leave much hope then, does it?"

Gene gently pushed her hair back over her shoulder. "Well, I'm thinking if he was your soulmate, then he wouldn't have succumbed to the dark things."

She looked up into his beautiful green eyes. "Maybe you're right," Jessica said, recalling the other clues. Remembering what she'd read in her diary, but unwilling to share. He might be her soulmate, but he wouldn't even admit to basic feelings for her, beyond the physical. She doubted he'd *ever* believe there could be more. His occasional 'jerk' attitude said everything he mouth didn't.

"Why don't you change into your pjs, and I'll see what I can do to help with that headache," he said.

Jessica raised an eyebrow.

"Hey! I meant I'd give you a massage. Get your mind out of the gutter."

She giggled. Pajamas weren't a bad idea—and neither were Gene's hands all over her body. She warmed, from the inside out.

He smacked her butt, and she yelped.

Jessica threw him a glare but couldn't quite be irked at his sexy smirk, or the twinkle in his eyes.

CHAPTER
EIGHTEEN

*Tom

Tom awoke when the light became too bright to ignore. He couldn't remember ever sleeping so well. The perfect way to start what would be a very long day.

Alex was still curled up in his arms, and he caressed the smooth skin of her back. She snuggled closer in her sleep, making soft moaning noises.

Tom wished he didn't have to leave her, but he had a job to do. He couldn't let that thing threaten her safety.

They had stopped in this small town for a reason.

The girls were a wonderful distraction, but it was time to get back to work.

He also didn't want to face what killing that thing meant. They'd move on to the next job and he'd never see Alex again.

Tom sighed, not wanting to leave. He could see himself helping her fix up this place and make it nice again.

Alex stirred and looked up at him, smiling sleepily. "Good morning."

"Good morning."

"Did you get some sleep?" she asked.

"I slept better than I ever have," Tom said.

Alex sat up, the sheet falling away from her bare body.

Tom appreciated the view.

"What time do you have to head out?" she asked, her expression changing to one of concern.

He sighed again. He didn't want to think of leaving her, but it was inevitable. "As soon as we can get ready."

Alex nodded. "How will you get out there? I didn't see any roads when we were out there?"

"We'll walk."

She wrinkled up her nose. "That's a long way to walk."

Tom shrugged.

"You could take the horses," she said.

"Thank you, but I wouldn't want something to happen to your horses."

"I don't want something to happen to *you*," she said, laying back down against him.

Tom held her tight. "Nothing's going to happen to me. I'll be back in time to have some more of that delicious potato salad we had at dinner last night."

Alex chuckled. "But what should we have with our potato salad?"

"Hmm, I'm thinking steak," Tom said.

"Oh, that sounds good. Jessica bought some steaks, but I'm not very good at grilling, though."

"That's all right. If you can get them ready, Gene will grill them. He loves that stuff."

They lay there quietly for a few minutes.

"Tom?"

"Hmm?"

"What if I ride out to the lake with you and drop you off? Then I can bring the horses back? That way, you don't have to walk so far."

"I don't really want you going all the way out to the lake, but I suppose it wouldn't hurt to get us closer."

"Then when you're ready, just call me, and we can come pick you up," Alex said.

Tom smiled yet again. She always made him smile. It was so sweet the way she wanted to help but was trying to stay out of the way so he could do what he needed to. "That sounds like a good idea. I'm sure Gene and I will be tired after the hunt."

"And if you find some victims, we can use the horses to get them out," she said, hope clearly resonating in her voice.

"Babe, I don't want you to get your hopes up that we'll find anyone."

She tilted her head back to look at him, a concerned crease in her brow. "Why not?"

"Because the last three people that went missing turned up eaten. That could mean that the others were already dead, and it was just looking for its next meal. The Wendigos gorge themselves but never get truly full, so they are always hunting," Tom said.

"But you said they store their victims, so there could be someone," her voice pleaded with him.

"It's a remote possibility. But the likelihood is those people are gone. And all we can do is prevent him from taking others," he said, running his finger through her hair to soften his honesty.

After a few heartbeats of silence, Alex's pretty face relaxed, but she took an audible breath. "I think I'll just pray that we can help someone."

"Well then, I'll hope for that, too."

Gene

Gene came downstairs and the scent of bacon frying wafted around him.

Jessica had slipped out of bed a few minutes before and headed to the shower, assuming he was still asleep.

He'd watched her go before he rolled out of bed. It'd been an oddly comfortable night. He'd massaged Jessica's neck and shoulders until she fell asleep, then he'd curled up with her and fallen asleep himself.

Gene wasn't used to spending the entire night with a woman. When he did, it was usually because they'd had sex. With her, he just felt…right, like he could simply be himself and she wouldn't mind.

The sound of movement downstairs had him up and dressed within a few minutes. The urgency to get the job done, kill the Wendigo, was gnawing at him. But so was the thought that they'd have to leave when the job was done.

He pushed open the swinging kitchen door.

"Morning, Gene," Tom said. His cousin sat at the small table with a full plate in front of him.

He threw his cousin a nod. "Mornin'."

"Have a seat, Gene. I'll have some breakfast for you in a jif," Alex said, smiling over her shoulder.

Gene obeyed, taking the chair next to Tom.

Alex brought him a glass of milk.

He wanted to protest, but the look on his cousin's face told him he better graciously accept. "Thanks," he said. He took a sip for good measure.

"So, Alex had a good idea," Tom said.

"Yeah?"

"She's going to ride in with us, so we don't have to walk all the way. She'll bring the horses back, then pick us up after."

Gene raised his eyebrows. "You really think that's a good idea? Horseback?"

"Have you ever ridden?" Alex asked.

"Have I ever ridden!" he said.

It was Tom's turn to arch an eyebrow, and his cousin smirked.

"Well, not really," Gene said hating to admit a weakness—or defeat.

"My horses are pretty easy for beginners, so you shouldn't have a problem," Alex said as she set a plate in front of Gene, full of pancakes, bacon, and a fried egg.

"Wow, this looks great!" His stomach growled in agreement.

"I can't have you going out there hungry," she said, heading back to the stove. She pulled all the fixings for sandwiches from the fridge and packed them a lunch.

Jessica came downstairs, wearing jeans and a T-shirt. She was still tying her hair in a ponytail when she came into the kitchen.

"Wow! I didn't know you even owned jeans!" Gene gaped.

"Of course I own jeans. Besides, I can't very well go tromping through the woods in a dress now, could I?"

"You are not going with us," he said, going for nonchalance, and back to his plate. He didn't want to argue, but he wouldn't bend on this.

"I want to help. This thing needs to be stopped," she said, stepping in front of him with her hands on her hips.

"I said no," Gene replied calmly, trying to hold it together, but heat was rising from his gut, warming his face.

"I can help. I'm sure you can use an extra pair of eyes and when we find the victims—"

"No!" he said, jumping to his feet, fueled by fear for her.

Jessica hopped back a step. "I have first aid training, and so does Alex." She gestured to her friend.

Gene glanced at Alex.

She held her hands up in surrender.

"Jessica, it's too dangerous for you. You're not going!" he commanded.

Tom stood and put one hand on Gene's chest and the other on Jessica's shoulder. "All right, you two, that's enough."

Jessica harrumphed and moved to Alex, her arms folded across her chest, and her cheeks red, in obvious indignation.

"Jessica, Gene and I've been hunting for a long time. We can anticipate what the other is going to do. When you add more people, that's when someone ends up getting hurt," Tom said, trying to diffuse the situation. His voice was calm, as was his expression. "We appreciate the offer, but it's too dangerous."

"Why don't you come with me to take the guys in closer, and you can help me bring the horses back? Then we can be ready, when or if they find some victims still alive. We can go help after they've taken care of the Wendigo," Alex suggested, handing Jessica a plate of food.

Her friend grumbled and took her plate to the table.

"I still don't see why I can't go," she protested again.

"Maybe he doesn't want you to get hurt," her bestie said.

"I won't get hurt. I have martial arts training, and I know how to shoot a gun."

"Jessica, this isn't about you. It's what they do. It's their job. Would you want Gene standing over your shoulder telling you that you were sewing a quilt wrong? No. You'd kick him out of your sewing room because you know what you're doing."

"Nice analogy," Gene pointed out, grabbing his plate from the table and depositing it by the sink. "Thank you for breakfast." He turned to head outside, Tom on his heels. He didn't get far when he noticed they weren't alone.

"If you don't want me to go, can I at least see what you're doing? I'm just curious," she said in a flat tone.

"Fine," her lover said.

Gene was impressed as she watched the preparations they were making and asked a few questions. Some were about hunting in general, and some about Wendigos specifically. He pointed out the weapons and tools they were packing.

Alex brought out the food she had made them to pack in their duffel. Neither Gene nor Tom had the heart to tell her there wouldn't be time for a picnic lunch.

CHAPTER
NINETEEN

Alex

Alex let Tom help her brush and saddle the horses. It was pretty impressive to her how much he'd remembered from the day before. He still asked questions, and she had to help him with the cinch, but it didn't take them long to get both horses ready.

He stepped up into Anduril's saddle, Alex joining behind him. She could feel the beating of his heart when she wrapped her arms around him.

She watched with pride as Jessica held Ellie for Gene, then slung herself up on the back of the saddle. She had taught Jessica how to ride.

"Uh, I don't know where I'm going?" Gene said awkwardly.

"It's okay," Jessica said, tightening her arms around him. "I'm pretty sure Ellie does." Ellie, of course, being a lead mare, wouldn't allow Anduril to stay in the lead for long, and she quickly trotted ahead.

Alex led them to the clearing where she and Tom had stopped to picnic. She let the horse drop his head to graze and when Tom swung his leg over so he wouldn't kick Alex as he got off.

Gene followed suit.

Alex and Jessica slipped forward into the saddles, while the guys grabbed their weapons out of their bags.

Tom looked up at her. "I'll call you when it's over and we'll try to meet you here."

"Be careful," she pleaded.

He crooked a finger at her, and Alex smiled.

She leaned over and kissed him.

"I expect another when I finish this." He winked as she straightened on the horse.

"Are you two done?" Gene said, sounding disgusted. "We've got a monster to hunt."

Jessica rolled her eyes.

Alex smirked. She had no regrets—only that the man she was starting to care a great deal about was going into danger. Her heart skipped and she glanced at Tom's tall form again, just as her bestie got snarky.

"You are such a guy. Why can't you let Alex and Tom have their moment?" Jessica swung out of the saddle and took a few steps over to Gene, grabbing his shirt with both hands, pulling him in, and kissed him passionately.

Tom's cousin didn't fight her, of course. He wrapped his arms around her and pulled her in tight.

Alex tried not to let the PDA affect her, but her cheeks rushed with heat. She might've kissed Tom, but Jessica and Gene took it to another level.

"Don't forget, you accepted my challenge and I expect you to make good on it tonight," Jessica teased before she sauntered back to Ellie and swung up in the saddle. "Good luck," she said, and whirled the mare back toward the house.

Alex smiled at Tom, but he could no doubt read the concern she couldn't hide. She needed to go back before she threw herself into his arms and begged him not to go. She urged Anduril after Ellie.

. . .

"By the way, what was that challenge?" Alex asked, trotting her horse closer to her bestie.

Jessica blushed to the tips of her ears. "It's nothing."

She smirked and shook her head. She wouldn't push her friend to voice the no doubt naughty plan for later.

They fell into silence, and only the clomp clomp of Ellie and Anduril's hooves were audible.

It'd do no good to worry about Tom, but she couldn't help it. She'd taken a college class about Native American history and was familiar with the legends of the Wendigo.

The images that had been created over the years were horrifying enough. She couldn't imagine what the real thing was like.

When they reached the house, they tied the horses to the horse trailer without unsaddling them.

Alex wanted to be ready when Tom called, so they loosened the cinches slightly and let the horses stand.

She stopped to get the first aid kit out of the horse trailer and the one out of the van.

Jessica

Jessica went inside to gather sheets they could cut up to use as bandages and see what other supplies Great Aunt Marge had around the house that might work. She checked the cupboards in the kitchen and found scissors and a box of Band-Aids. She tried to think of where else someone might keep stuff.

"Cellar."

The voice drifted to her.

She looked around, "Grams?" she asked.

"Out the back." The voice came again.

Jessica obeyed this time and went out the back door. She found the storm shelter door and pulled it open. She descended into the darkness, and she didn't have a flashlight. "Is there a light?"

"Left," came the voice.

Was she really talking to a ghost?

She found a chain and pulled it, clicking on the overhead light. It was comprised of two bare lightbulbs, but it was sufficient light for the small room.

There were shelves on one wall that were full of supplies. Everything from non-perishable food and water to medical supplies and blankets.

"Wow! Thanks, Grams!"

She took an armful of medical stuff up to the dining room and spread it all out so they could see what they had, but also to get her mind in the moment.

Jessica was obsessing about Gene. She wanted him to be safe. The fortune teller danced into her head again.

She couldn't deny the physical attraction they had, and yet it was more than that. Jessica felt connected to him somehow. She couldn't explain it.

Maybe it was just the idea of him being her soulmate that had her thinking all this in the first place. Of course, she didn't have a clue how he truly felt about her. He sent such mixed signals. Not to mention, they hadn't known each other long.

Alex came down the stairs. "There you are! I just checked the bathroom but only found a few little things. Where did you find all this?" She gestured to the table.

"In the storm shelter," Jessica said.

"What made you think to look there?"

"Grams told me." She smiled.

"Grams? So now you're okay with a ghost living with us?"

Jessica shrugged. "She's only been helpful, right?"

Her bestie cocked her head to one side, but nodded.

"And technically, we live with her. Judith and George built this house."

Alex shook her head. "You're right, of course, but somehow it doesn't feel right. It's like your great-great-grandmother's trapped here and just trying to make the best of it."

"Maybe."

They packed as much of the supplies into the saddlebags as possible, just in case Tom called and needed help.

The sun was glaring down on them while they worked.

"Damn, my head aches. I think we've done all we can do, so now we just need to wait," Alex said.

They returned to the house.

Jessica turned on her guilty pleasure music, Razor's Edge, but quickly shut it off. It seemed to be causing Alex's head to pound worse than it already was.

Her friend got severe headaches when she was stressed out.

"Uh, oh. I've seen that look before," she said.

"I know, not a great time for a migraine. If I just go lay down in the quiet for a while, it should be gone by the time Tom calls," Alex said.

"Good idea," Jessica said.

Her bestie retrieved some meds, grabbed some ice, and went to her room.

Jessica was going to seize the opportunity. She had no intention of staying home while the boys hunted.

She'd planned to join them as soon as she could get Alex distracted, so this worked to her advantage.

Jessica went into her room to get her favorite button-up flannel shirt. She grabbed an over-the-shoulder satchel and her 9mm handgun, then quietly slipped out of the house.

Alex didn't know about the gun, but Jessica was licensed to carry and a damn excellent shot. She stopped at the van and got her road flares out of her emergency kit, putting them in her bag. She untied Ellie, leading the horse away from the house before mounting.

Jessica glanced at the house one last time before heading for the lake.

Alex would be safe at home.

But she couldn't sit by idly.

Something knawed inside her, telling her she *needed* to be with the guys.

The horse made it to the clearing where they'd dropped the guys off in record time.

Jessica left Ellie with her reins looped over her head but didn't tie her up. The mare needed the opportunity to escape if something happened.

She transferred some of the first aid supplies from the saddlebags to her satchel, moving her flares to the top. She stuffed the gun in the back of the waistband of her jeans and glanced across the clearing.

That was the direction the guys had headed.

Jessica spotted a path they'd cut through the tall grass. She took a deep breath, steeling herself before setting off.

She made good time, coming out at the lake just in time to see Gene and Tom move into the trees on the north side.

Jessica huffed in frustration. It was a long way around the lake, but they had a pretty good head start on her.

She slipped her satchel off her shoulder to carry it in her hands and began jogging around the lake, trying to catch up as quickly as possible.

CHAPTER
TWENTY

Gene

Gene and Tom hiked toward the lake in silence. They were both on high alert, keeping their eyes open for the Wendigo. They ended up by the lake, in the same spot Tom and Alex had the day before.

"Any idea which way to go now?" he asked his cousin.

Tom surveyed the lake. "The victims they found were all on the north side of the lake. May as well start there."

"Why do you think he left some?" Gene asked as they started hiking.

"Don't know. Got interrupted maybe?"

"Or he was playing with his food," he said morbidly. Gene froze as he heard twigs snapping behind him. He spun and pointed his flare gun at the trees.

Jessica came through the brush. She was breathing hard from running but froze when she spotted the flare gun pointed at her.

"Dammit, Jessica!" he yelled. "What the hell are you doing here?" He dropped his aim, and she rushed to his side.

"I didn't want to let you boys have all the fun." She smiled, still trying to catch her breath.

"Jessica, it's dangerous out here."

"I know that, Gene. I'm not stupid, but I want that thing dead, too. I figured if you guys could use all the help you could get," she said, her shoulders stiff with obvious determination. "Besides, you said we might find some victims, and I brought some first aid supplies."

Gene glanced at Tom, hoping his cousin would say something that would convince Jessica to go back.

Tom shrugged.

Neither of them seemed to know what to say to make Jessica go back.

"Where's Alex?" Tom asked, his brow drawn in worry.

"She's home resting. She got a migraine, so I left after she laid down."

"I didn't know whether to be relieved to know that Alex is home safe or worried that she has a migraine," he whispered.

"She'll be fine. She'd been getting them for years."

Gene growled. He grabbed Jessica's arm and started pulling her back the way they'd come. "And you'll be fine once you get the hell outta here and go back home!"

She dropped the bag she was carrying and planted her feet. "No. I'm coming with you. I need to be here."

He wrapped an arm around her middle and picked her up, moving her in front of him.

As soon as her feet touched the ground, she leaned forward quickly, pulling him off his feet and flipping him to the ground in front of her.

Gene hit the ground with a soft thud that knocked the wind out of him.

"I said no!" she shouted.

She had a half-crazed look in her eyes. It was as if, in her mind, it wasn't him she'd just thrown to the ground, but someone who was trying to hurt her.

He lay still, trying to catch his breath.

"Jessica, take it easy," Tom said, holding his hands out like he was trying to calm an angry dog.

She whipped around, glaring at him. "I won't let anyone hurt me ever again," she said through gritted teeth.

"We're not gonna hurt you," his cousin said calmly, dropping his hands to his sides, "But this Wendigo will."

"I've had self-defense training," Jessica said.

"A Wendigo isn't going to be slowed down by that," Tom said.

Gene slowly rose to his feet behind her. "It doesn't matter now, Tom. She's here and the only way to make sure she stays safe is to keep her with us."

Jessica lifted her chin when she met his eyes. "Damn straight."

He stepped close, invading her personal space. "Jessica, I don't want you here." He kept his voice hard. "I don't want you to get hurt, but you're so stubborn you've risked not only your life but mine and Tom's as well. So, I hope you enjoy the thrill of the hunt because you could get us all killed." He walked past her and started making his way through the woods again.

Jessica hurried after him. "I know I'm tough. I had to be after what Justin had done to me. I just want to help. I didn't think it would make it harder on you guys."

"It doesn't matter now," Gene said. "Stay between Tom and I and do everything we say."

She nodded and got quiet.

He didn't look at it, and he couldn't give in to his panic at the idea of her getting hurt. Anger and worry warred in his gut.

Gene needed to focus on the monster they were hunting and manage to keep all three of them alive.

They spent another hour tramping through the woods.

"So, what does this thing look like?" Jessica asked.

"Shh!" Gene hissed over his shoulder at her.

Tom moved up close to her and whispered, "Just watch for movement," he said. "Wendigos are fast, so you won't see it before it's on you."

Gene kept going and he was twenty steps ahead of them. He held up a hand to stop Tom and Jessica.

Tom gripped her shoulder, pulling her to a halt.

They waited while Gene scouted around.

"Here!" he called.

The trail had wound through the woods and turned back down toward the lake. There was fresh blood on the trail where Gene had stopped.

It was still wet, so it had to be recent.

They all exchanged a look and continued silently down the trail.

At a bend in the trail, he stopped again, and Jessica bumped into him. He scowled.

Around the trees, there were some large rocky hills, and in the side of one hill was a cave. It looked like more of a crack in the rock, but it was big enough for a person to get through.

Gene set down the duffel and pulled the extra flares out, handing some to Tom. He pulled out a road flare and handed it to Jessica. "You stay here. If he comes out, use this to keep him away from you. We should be right behind him."

She opened her satchel and pulled out a handful of road flares and a gun.

He was reluctantly impressed. Still wished she was safe at the house, with Alex.

"How do you know he's in there?" she asked.

"We don't," Tom said. "It's gonna be dark in there and there's no telling if it's just one cave or a network."

Jessica nodded and pulled a flashlight out of her bag, handing it to Gene. "Good luck." She grabbed his sleeve. "What do I do if he comes out here?"

Part of him was glad she was scared and the other part just wanted to protect her. "Light a flare and keep the fire pointed at him," he said. "It's like a bear or a lion. They're afraid of fire, but he's faster too, so be on guard. Your gun won't stop him, but it may slow him down. Keep it close. Aim for the eyes or the knees if you can. And keep your eyes peeled. He may not be in there and could sneak up on you."

She started to shake. "I thought I was braver than this, but now when it comes down to it, I'm realizing this monster could kill us all."

Gene caressed her cheek. "It's going to be all right. Tom and I will take care of it." He kissed her quickly and headed into the cave.

He moved forward, his cousin at his side. They each held a flashlight in one hand and a flare gun in the other.

The entrance widened out, allowing them to walk side-by-side as the ground sloped downward.

Tom's feet slid under him as the slope dropped abruptly.

Rocks and debris crumbled and tumbled downward, tinking off the sides of the decline.

Gene grabbed his arm to stop him from falling on his ass.

"Help, is somebody there?"

It was a woman's voice.

Gene exchanged a look with his cousin.

It could be a trap.

Wendigos could mimic voices.

The tunnel veered off toward the left. Tom took the lead since he was closer.

Something suddenly threw him against the wall.

Gene heard Tom's clothes and flesh ripping as his cousin screamed.

He shot at the creature, but it dodged the flare.

The cave lit for a moment.

Tom was crumpled against the wall of the cave.

The Wendigo stood over his bloodied cousin, turned, and glared at Gene.

He had to get it away from Tom.

Gene fired a second flare, then ran for the entrance.

The creature screamed as the flare hit its arm. It pursued him back toward the cave entrance.

Gene ran with all his strength, losing ground when he got to the slippery incline.

The monster made a grab for him, shredding his shirt and shoulder.

He pulled a road flare and struck it, holding it at arm's length from the creature, until he could get on his feet.

The Wendigo growled and Gene took off again, throwing the flare in the creature's face.

Jessica

Jessica stood outside the cave behind a tree, watching. She'd pulled the rest of her flares out and waited. Her fingers were aching from her grip on them when she heard noises coming from the cave.

Gene was yelling and it sounded like he was scrambling around.

A couple of flashes followed the sound of the flare gun from inside the cave.

Her heart pounded when she heard screaming.

"Gene!" Jessica yelled. She wanted to help him, but she'd promised to wait. If she ran in now, she could distract him from making the killing shot. She shifted her weight back and forth on her feet, in agitation as she strained to hear anything else.

Gene came out of the cave at a full run. He moved toward the lake, away from Jessica, as he dodged behind a tree.

Something was right behind him.

The creature wasn't quite what she was expecting. It was taller than Gene and probably would tower over Tom as well. The skin of the monster was gray, and every inch was exposed. It didn't have a stitch of cloth anywhere on the body. It looked like it had chewed on its lips until there was nothing left. The teeth were rotten and jagged and she could smell its horrible breath even from the distance they were.

Jessica shifted her eyes back to Gene.

He was already bloody.

Her eyes darted back to the cave entrance. Surely, Tom would be right behind them and kill the thing.

Tom didn't come out.

Gene took a shot at the Wendigo, but it dodged and came for him again.

Jessica couldn't wait anymore.

She pulled out her gun and shot the Wendigo.

The bullet hit its right leg, just above the knee.

The Wendigo turned to her. Its eyes were a weird shade of yellow. It bared rotten teeth at her and snarled.

Jessica gasped as it took a step toward her.

"No!" Gene yelled. He threw himself forward and plunged a knife into the creature's back.

The Wendigo screamed and focused on the man who'd just stabbed it. It lashed out, knocking Gene into a tree.

He lay there, stunned.

Jessica scooped up her flares and struck one. She ran toward them.

The Wendigo shook like a dog, freeing the knife from his back, then stalked toward Gene.

It was going to pounce on him.

Jessica threw her flare. It hit the back of its bald head.

"Jessica, no!" Gene yelled as the Wendigo looked at Jessica again.

She was in the moment. Her fear forgotten; she needed to stop the thing from killing Gene.

Jessica charged the monster and she lit another flare.

The Wendigo growled, its pointed teeth bared, yellow eyes narrowed to slits as it came to meet her.

She threw the flare in its face, temporarily blinding it.

Gene shot off another flare.

Jessica skidded to a halt as the beast's body glowed red from the chest for a moment before it burst into flames.

It screamed as it died.

She watched the creature disintegrate in front of her.

Gene was still on the ground behind the Wendigo.

Jessica skirted the fiery mess to get to him.

He had an arm wrapped across his ribs and was struggling to get to his feet.

"Gene, are you all right?" She slid onto her knees beside him. She pulled his head and shoulders onto her lap.

He collapsed back onto her lap. "Tom," was all he said before he passed out.

CHAPTER
TWENTY-ONE

*Alex

"Tom!" Alex screamed as she sat bolt upright in bed. Her headache was suddenly gone, and her thinking was clear. Her only thought was that Tom needed her right now.

She jumped out of her bed and ran for the door.

"Jessica!" she cried as she ran down the stairs.

Her boots were by the front door, and she pulled them on as she moved outside. "Jessica! We gotta go!" she yelled again.

She listened as she grabbed her hoodie off the coat rack. There was nothing but silence.

Alex pulled the door open and stepped out onto the porch. Ellie was gone. She cursed under her breath.

She should've known that Jessica would take off after the guys.

Alex ran over to Anduril, vaulted onto the tall horse without tightening the saddle, and took off at a dead run.

She rode straight to the clearing.

Ellie was there, grazing. Her mare looked up and whinnied, trotting over to them.

Alex grabbed her reins without dismounting, and guided the gelding toward the lake, traveling as fast as the foliage would allow.

Ellie kept up without complaint.

Countless trees slapped Alex's face, leaving cuts and scrapes, but she didn't care. She had to get to Tom as quickly as possible. She was being drawn to him but didn't have time to worry about why.

She raced Anduril around the lake at a full gallop. She was almost halfway around when something inside told her to turn into the trees.

Alex broke through to the rocky hillside.

Gene was on the ground covered in blood, his head in Jessica's lap.

There was a burning pile not twenty feet from them.

The horses shied away from the sickening smell.

Alex swung out of the saddle. "Is he alive?" she called to Jessica.

"Yeah. How did you find us?"

Alex didn't answer.

She unclipped her saddlebags and ran into the cave before her friend had finished her sentence.

It was dark inside, but Alex made her way toward Tom. She watched her footing as she descended into the darkness. Her heart raced, but she could feel that she was getting closer to him.

Her flashlight finally crossed over him.

Her lover was crumpled against the wall, his face down, bloody, and his clothes torn to shreds.

Alex dropped the saddlebags and pulled him away from the wall, rolling him on his back.

He was heavy, but she had adrenalin on her side and she got him turned over.

She leaned down and listened to his chest.

His heart was beating, but his breath was coming in wet, raspy breaths.

"Hold on Tom, I got you," Alex said. She dumped the supplies out next to him and began searching for the worst wounds.

He had deep scratches across his chest that were bleeding profusely.

She pressed a clean towel and applied some pressure. She'd packed needles and thread for stitching up cuts, but these were deep and even if she stitched him closed, he could continue to bleed internally.

Alex had to get him out of there, but she couldn't move him like he was. She had some gauze, but she was convinced she could lift him on her own.

"Tom!" Gene's rough voice came through the darkness.

Relief washed through her.

Gene could help her get him out. Although Tom was taller, Gene was also over six feet tall and they were both solid muscle.

"Gene! We're over here!"

A flashlight bobbed toward her.

Tom started to cough, and her flashlight beam told her it was full of bloody spittle.

"No! Tom, hold on!" Alex cried, and her tears fell on his chest.

Tom groaned quietly, his eyes opening slightly.

"Please God, don't let him leave me," Alex begged.

Tom

Tom looked up into Alex's dark eyes and tried to reach for her, but he was too weak.

Jessica stepped up behind her best friend, knelt down, and placed her hands on her shoulder. "It's going to be okay, Alex. He has to be all right. He has to be…" She rested her forehead on the top of Alex's head, surely trying to hide tears.

Don't cry for me. I'm going out doing what I love…

He was unable to find the energy to speak the plea.

Suddenly, Alex's eyes gave off a light, quickly going radiant, the orbs illuminating from within. Glowing.

The warm, golden color spread through her body. As it reached her fingers, it surged into him.

Tom felt a warmth, as if she was soothing his soul. It spread from her hands, traveling to all of his injuries, soothing and healing them.

The light spread around them, becoming so bright that Gene and Jessica had to shield their eyes.

He gasped, and the light faded.

When his vision adjusted to the newly dim cave, Tom glanced at a figure standing behind Alex.

A beautiful woman with ebony curly hair and aquamarine eyes, dressed in a brown leather bustier and green flowing skirt that reminded him of the color of pine stood there. Her feet were bare. She had a beautiful green filigree tattoo traveling up her arm and over her shoulders that reminded him of vines. His eyes traveled up to see her hand was on Jessica's shoulder.

Tom reached up and touched Alex's wet cheek. All the small scrapes she'd had moments before were gone.

She leaned into his palm, her blood-covered hand coming up to his.

"Alex, how did you—" He owed his life to her, even though he wasn't certain what exactly had happened.

"Tom, you're all right!" she cried.

Gene

"Who is that?" Jessica asked Gene, rising from Alex's side, and stepping closer to him.

He draped his good arm over her shoulders, so she could help him stand. The Wendigo had broken some ribs and torn the muscles in his left shoulder. Pain radiated all over his body, and he gritted his teeth so he wouldn't show it, and so he could speak.

Alex whirled. It was clear she'd just noticed the woman standing behind her. Then she protectively stretched to cover as much of Tom as she could with her body.

Gene looked back at the newcomer.

She was breathtaking yet intimidating. "Don't worry, I won't hurt him," she said in a sing-song voice.

Tom pushed himself up to a sitting position behind Alex. "Why?" he whispered, but his voice was curious, and knowing his cousin, not ungrateful for the help.

"I had to come when I heard Jade's call through my kin," the woman said.

"Jade?" Tom asked, his voice wavering.

Even in the darkness of the cave, Gene didn't miss Alex's blush of obvious embarrassment.

He glanced at the woman. "We didn't call you, whoever the hell you are," Gene said.

"She did," the newcomer pointed at Alex. "She called for help, and through my kin, I heard, and so I answered. But now I must return to my duties."

"Who are you? And not that we don't appreciate the help, but why?" Gene asked. Gene stepped away from Jessica, closer to the woman, ready to demand answers she didn't seem forthcoming with.

Before he could speak, the stranger put two fingers on his forehead.

Heat radiated through his body, and he felt each rib move back into place, each torn muscle stitching itself back together.

He slid away from the woman, rubbing his arm.

It felt as good as new.

Gene's eyes skipped over Jessica, Alex, and Tom.

They all wore identical amazed expressions.

The monster had torn his arm shreds; he'd been convinced he'd never be able to use it again. That hadn't been his only injury.

He'd been limping and having trouble breathing. He'd hobbled into the cave with sheer adrenaline to get to Tom.

Now, even the cuts on his face were gone.

"I must return. I'm needed elsewhere," the woman said to Gene, her voice was like the sound of tinkling bells. She looked back at Alex. "It was your love that saved him," she told her, before turning to Jessica. "Your love for your friend allowed *us* to heal him."

"Us?" Alex said.

"Love is a powerful thing, especially when true love is involved. Hold on to that and know that you all have very important things to do. Besides, it wasn't written for him to die today," she said.

"You're a… a …" Gene said, grasping at straws, trying to put his finger on what exactly she was. They'd hunted just about every preternatural creature, yet he was drawing a blank on this being.

"Not ready to share that information. You have had very little interaction with our kind, Gene Priest. You will learn soon enough. But like I said, it wasn't written for him to die today. There is something coming, Tom, Gene." She looked at each of them when she said their names. "Be ready," she commanded, and then she disappeared.

Alex gasped.

"What the hell!" Jessica cried.

"Where did she go?"

"Dammit!" Gene cursed under his breath.

Jessica grabbed his right arm. "Who was that?"

"I have no idea," Tom said, but he looked at Alex.

"What creature has the power to do that? I thought all paranormal stuff was bad. They take lives, not give them," Alex said.

"I've heard stories about things like Wish-Granters and Fayefolk. We hunt Wendigos and vampires, but it's hard to believe some of the others out there. And I've never heard about one giving a life back," Tom said.

"Yeah, well. I still don't like that she said something's coming. No shit. Something is always coming," Gene huffed. He was trying to let her *other* words blow over him.

True Love.

She'd said their true love gave them the power to heal Tom. He'd seen the movie *Frozen* - it was the only thing on TV one night - so he knew true love could be a platonic thing between sisters. Maybe that's what she meant. The love Jessica and Alex held for each other.

Yeah.

Because that wasn't something *he'd* ever have.

"Why did she call you Jade?" Tom asked Alex, breaking Gene's inner tirade.

"Because that's my name," she said.

"I thought your name was Alex."

"It is," Jessica said.

Gene exchanged a look with his cousin, not missing Tom's enlarged orbs.

Jessica sighed. "After what happened with Justin, I needed a fresh start, so I moved from Oregon to Colorado and started going by my middle name. New life, new name. Alex has been my best friend since we were ten. We've done just about everything together. So when I decided to make a major change, she joined me. Name change and all."

"So, what's your first name?" Gene asked Jessica.

"Em," she replied.

Alex coughed. "Tell the truth."

"Fine!" She huffed, crossing her arms. "Emily."

"Emily? What's so wrong about that?" Gene smirked and snorted.

Jessica rolled her eyes. "Pretty much every other girl in school was named Emily."

A sound broke their conversation and had Tom climbing to his feet. "Did you hear that?"

"Yeah, I don't think we're alone," Gene said, pulling the knife out of his jacket.

"Is it another Wendigo?" Alex asked, slipping closer to Tom.

"No, Wendigos live alone," he said, grabbing her hand.

"But you said that some of the missing people might be alive," Jessica said as she shined her flashlight around.

They heard the sound again.

It was a cry, but like someone with a gag in their mouth.

Gene took the lead and headed deeper into the cave with Jessica on his heels.

Tom picked up his flare gun and shoved it in his belt, then grabbed Alex's flashlight in his left hand and held her hand in his right.

They followed Gene and Jessica to a bend deep underground.

The room opened a little and there they found bodies strung up by their hands and gags in their mouths.

One person was moving, and Jessica dashed over to him. She pulled the gag out of his mouth. "It's all right. We're here to help."

"Run! Monster!" he said, struggling for breath.

Gene used his knife to cut the man down.

"It's dead now," Jessica told the man as he collapsed onto her. She pulled out her pocket knife and started cutting off his bindings.

Gene helped move him to a sitting position while Tom and Alex checked the others.

They found four other victims still alive.

Two of the men were unconscious and badly injured.

"What do we do now?" Jessica asked.

"We have to get them out of here first," Alex said. Her take-charge manner surprised Gene. "Tom, can you and Gene carry these guys out of here?"

"Yeah, sure, but it is a long way back to the farm," Tom said.

"First things, first. You get the guys out and Jessica and I will get the two girls." Alex walked over to the closest girl. She was filthy, with short black hair and a thin frame. "Come on, let's get you out of here." She slipped an arm under the girl.

Jessica helped get her up, and the three of them started moving toward the entrance.

Gene glanced at his cousin.

Tom wore a look of surprise and helped him pick up the conscious man.

They each put one of the guy's arms around their shoulders and helped him out.

Although he was a big guy, Tom still had to hunch over a little to help him.

The man tried to walk as much as he could.

"How did you find us?" he asked hoarsely.

"Just lucky," Gene said.

"How long have you been here?" Tom asked.

"I don't know. My girlfriend and I went on a picnic to the lake. I was going to propose, but that thing..."

"What day was that?" Tom asked, getting the man back on track.

"Saturday."

Gene and Tom exchanged another look.

It was Thursday, so they'd been captive for five days. As they stepped out into the light, they all blinked at the brightness.

Gene spotted Jessica, with the girl sitting on the side of the clearing, as far away from the smoldering pile as possible.

They brought the man over and sat him next to her.

The two embraced.

Gene smiled.

Obviously, she was the woman the man had been talking about.

Alex went back to the horses to get some water bottles that she'd packed in Ellie's pack. She opened them and handed them to the victims.

They eagerly took the bottles and both sipped and then chugged.

"Can you guys bring the others up?" Alex asked.

Gene nodded, and his cousin echoed it.

"Great! Jessica, see if you can get a signal and call in some help."

"Where do I tell them we are?" she asked.

"Have them meet us at the farm. We'll need a couple of ambulances," Alex said, going back over to Anduril and Ellie.

"How do we get them all back?" Gene asked.

"We improvise," Alex said. She opened Ellie's saddlebag and pulled out a small hatchet. "You go get the others. I've got some work to do."

CHAPTER
TWENTY-TWO

*Alex

Alex found a few small ash trees and cut four of them down. She grabbed two and started dragging them back to the horses. At the edge of the clearing, she stripped them of the branches.

She retrieved some rope from her saddlebag and tied two of the ends together creating a travois. She tested the strength and when this satisfied her; she fetched the other two trees and began the process again.

Jessica came back with her phone in her hand. "Okay, I had to walk part way around the lake, but I finally got a signal, and they are sending help to the farm. Now what can I do?"

Tom and Gene emerged from the cave with one of the unconscious men.

"Help them settle him on that," Alex said, pointing at the litter.

The guys each had an arm under the man, with just his feet dragging the ground, but Jessica still had to help them get him prone on the litter.

Tom wiped his brow. "You built that?"

"Yeah," Alex said, glancing up from where she knelt next to the trees.

"Where did you learn to do this?"

"I was a mounted forest ranger in Colorado." She shrugged. "Now go get those other two so we can get the heck out of here."

Tom and Gene soon returned with the third guy and placed him on the second litter.

Gene made one last trip into the Wendigo's den to fetch the other girl.

Jessica and Alex tried to get some water into the unconscious men and treat some of their wounds, while Tom tightened the saddles.

Alex checked on the first couple they had brought out. "Do you think either of you could walk back to my farm?"

"I can," the man replied. "She'll need help, though."

Gene returned with the last girl, and Alex had him bring her over to Anduril. She helped the injured girl into the saddle, but she could hardly sit up.

Alex wasn't strong enough to hold the girl up *and* control the horse. She turned to Gene. "You'll have to get up behind her."

Gene seemed like he was searching for some excuse. It was obvious that he was already uncomfortable with the way the girl had referred to him as her hero, when he'd carried her out of the cave. He probably didn't want to be stuck on the back of a horse with her. "What about Betty?" he asked, pointing at the brunette that Tom was helping up. "Can't they ride together?"

Alex frowned. "No. This girl needs someone strong to hold her up. Get your ass up there!"

"Yes, ma'am," Gene smirked, but reluctance was still coming from him.

"Tom, Gene needs a leg up!" Alex called.

Her love left the brunette with Jessica and helped his cousin, and Alex balanced the girl.

When Gene was settled, he wrapped his arms around the girl to hold her in place.

Jessica led the brunette over to Ellie. She helped her up, as Alex walked over to assist her.

"Is she all right?"

"Yeah," her bestie said.

"I think that's her boyfriend. We should see if he can double up," Alex said, gesturing to the man Tom was helping get to his feet.

Tom helped boost the guy up behind his girlfriend on the horse, and got them settled.

"Okay, I'm going to take Ellie and head back. Jessica, I need you to walk behind Ellie and stop me if he starts to slide off," Alex pointed to the man on Ellie's travois. "Tom, I need you to walk behind Anduril and do the same. Gene, if she slips and you need me to stop, just tell Jessica. We need to go slow 'cause these aren't the sturdiest sleds." She took the lead. "Let's move out!"

She led Ellie around the still-smoldering pile and out to the lake. They all breathed a little easier when they were out of sight of the home of the Wendigo.

Jessica

Jessica glanced back at Gene.

The victim girl was leaning back against him, and he had his arms wrapped around her.

She was safely tucked in his embrace, and Jessica's heart soared.

Gene was showing so much kindness, even if he didn't realize it. This poor girl had been bound and almost some monster's meal and now she was being held by a man who was usually rougher around the edges. How many times had he been someone's savior? He played a tough guy, but here, now, she only saw the softer, caring side of him.

"Alex, stop!" Tom called, halting their little caravan.

Alex dropped Ellie's reins, reassuring the horse to wait, and jogged back. The man on the back sled had awakened and was fighting his restraints.

"I've got this," Jessica said. She was closest and got to him the fastest. "Hey, hey, hey easy there, buddy."

The man's dark brown eyes finally focused when she knelt next to him.

"It's all right. We are going to get you some help, okay?" she said.

"The beast," he breathed.

"It's dead," Tom said.

The man jerked violently, trying to get away from Tom.

Jessica gripped the man's shoulders. Her touch seemed to quickly calm him. "It's okay. He's here to help us. We're just trying to get back to the road so the ambulance can pick you up." She held his gaze while the words soaked in. When his breathing slowed, she continued. "Tom, here, is going to keep an eye out and make sure we don't lose anybody on the road, okay? So, he'll be back here with you."

The man nodded and grabbed her wrist.

She knelt back down to listen.

"It's really dead?" he asked, his eyes raking her face.

Jessica smiled. "Yes sir, it is."

He relaxed back onto the sled.

It was late afternoon when the farm came back into view. Relief washed over Jessica, and it was also reflected in the expressions around her.

It'd taken over an hour to get back at the slow pace they'd be forced to maintain, but they didn't want to rush and hurt the victims worse.

The paramedics ran toward them as soon as they came into view.

"What do we have?" one paramedic asked.

"I think the man on this sled is still unconscious, but the rest are awake and can tell you where they hurt. They are all dehydrated and hungry. The couple on this horse have minor injuries, but we've got a tourniquet on the unconscious man," Jessica said.

Alex pulled the horses to a stop, and there was a flurry of activity as the teams of paramedics assessed the victims.

One ambulance took off almost immediately with the two men who had been on the sleds. The other medical vehicle took the other couple, but they had to wait until they could pry the remaining girl off of Gene. She kept crying that she needed him to go with her and it took two paramedics to pull the girl's arms off of him.

Gene

Gene straightened his clothes as he went to the porch, where Tom was standing.

They usually cleared out before the authorities could question them, because that never ended well.

"Where are the girls?" he asked.

"Inside. The sheriff is in with them," his cousin said, watching the ambulance pull out.

Gene sighed and sat on the porch steps. It might be good to know what Jessica and Alex were telling the sheriff. Tomorrow they'd find Grandma's bones, salt and burn them, setting her free, and then they'd be on the road again.

Somehow, that left him feeling empty. He tried to convince himself he was just hungry, but deep down, he knew that wasn't it.

"Odd I know, but let's head in; see if they're covering our asses."

• • •

Gene and his cousin silently slipped into the house, stopping at the entryway to the living room. They leaned against the opposite sides of the door jamb.

The local sheriff was sitting on the edge of the chair next to the sofa, where Alex and Jessica were sitting. He was a stout older man, way past retirement age.

"Well, looks like all these folks were trespassing on your land. Do you want to press charges?"

"Why would I want to press charges?" Jessica asked, her eyes wide.

"Well, I know for certain that Rich and Mark, two of the victims, knew it was illegal to be fishing at the lake," the sheriff said.

"Why is it illegal?" Alex asked.

"Well, technically, the lake is on your land. Marge usually let people fish there if they asked permission. But she got concerned when she began hearing gunfire out there. Thought people were poaching, it was just easier to cut it off and not let anyone out there, especially after Marge went downhill. People still sneak out here from time to time and we have to run them off. For years, folks go missing, some leave this small town, and others just disappear. But lately, some of their things were turning up in this area. We suspected there was something going on. Wasn't until Beau, your neighbor up the road, went for his daily run and found the first body that we knew for sure there was something scary out there."

Gene exchanged a look with Tom.

"We have a neighbor?" Jessica asked.

"Yeah, he lives a couple of miles up the road, if you need any help. He's pretty handy at fixing things. He used to help your aunt out," he said, rising to his feet.

"How did you know Marge was my aunt?" Jessica asked.

He smiled. "You're the spittin' image of *her* mother, Edith."

"You knew my family?" Her eyes were still wide, her pretty face stamped with surprise.

The sheriff rubbed his thin, gray goatee. "Mostly Margie. I wanted to marry that girl. I courted her for so long that I got to know her family well. Her momma even approved of me, which was rare. That lady had twinkling aquamarine eyes, like yours and an attitude to match. But Margie, you see, she didn't want to get married. Ever."

"I'm sorry, Sheriff. Was she in love with someone else?" Alex asked as she and Jessica stood to walk him out.

"Nah. It wasn't like that. She loved me. And I loved her. But she never wanted to leave her home and marriage would surely make that happen. She also shared with me she never wanted kids. She'd said her Jessica was all she needed, that she'd carry the line. I never understood what she meant by that." He trailed off.

"Well, I'm Jessica. Maybe that's what she meant, although I only met her once when I was little, and I didn't start going by my middle name until a few years ago."

He smiled. "I doubt she was talking about a niece your age, honey. This was back in the 1950s. You weren't born yet." He took another step toward the door.

Gene made his way to the porch, his cousin behind him.

The sheriff was loud enough to still be heard through the screen door.

"Well, I best be heading out. Gotta stop at the hospital and get statements, then I'll have quite the report to fill out. I still can't believe you kids killed that rabid bear. I wish you hadn't burned it though. They're gonna wanna run tests."

"Sorry, sheriff," Gene heard Jessica say. "One of the guys shot it with a flare gun. It went straight into its chest and blew the creature up. Couldn't have stopped it from burning if we tried."

They all stepped out onto the porch.

Gene and Tom were sitting in the rocking chairs watching the sunset.

"You boys take care of these girls," the lawman said, eyeing Gene, then Tom, before turning back to Jessica and Alex. "If you need anything, you have my number." He went to his car and stopped with the cruiser door open. "Ya know, I think Marge would have enjoyed knowing you were here." He smiled and got in his car.

Gene stood up and clapped his hands together and simply said, "Food!"

CHAPTER
TWENTY-THREE

*Jessica

All eyes landed on Gene.

It might be just an ordinary day for him, but Jessica and her best friend were still dealing with their first hunt.

"How about we head down to that bar we met at and let someone else do the cooking tonight?" Tom broke the tension.

"Yeah, I could use a drink or three," Jessica said.

"But they don't have pie," Gene said with a pout.

"I'm sure you'll manage." Tom chuckled. "I'll never understand your obsession with pie."

"All right, but you need a shower before we go," Jessica said, gesturing at his clothes.

Gene looked down at himself. His clothing was still covered in blood. "What, you don't think we should go all decorated in red gore?" He smirked.

Alex glanced at Tom.

"It wouldn't be the first time." He shrugged.

"Well, I, for one, don't want a reminder of what that beast did to you," Jessica said.

Gene shrugged. "Not my worst injury."

"Ugh! Gene, I don't want to hear that!" she said, throwing her hands up.

"Well, we could all use a shower," Alex said, pulling open the screen door. "Jessica, if you plan on washing your hair, you better go first. And I recommend you wash your hair."

Jessica sighed. Even with a blow dryer, her hair was so thick she usually gave up before it was even remotely dry. If she showered before bed, it was always still damp in the morning.

She headed upstairs and jumped in the shower, trying to keep it quick so everyone else had some hot water, too.

Jessica left the bathroom with just a towel. She knocked on Gene's door to let him know he was next.

His pretty green eyes were obviously lust-filled, because the towel barely covered her long, curvy body.

She smiled back at him, but dodged when he reached for her. She needed to get dressed, and knew exactly what she wanted to wear.

Jessica heard Gene take a quick shower. She'd kept her door open, hoping to catch a glimpse of him coming out. Sure enough, the creak of the bathroom door had her peering out into the hall.

He also only had a towel wrapped around his slim waist, water trailing down his smooth chest.

She licked her lips as she headed to Alex's door.

Jessica could feel Gene's eyes on her, so she glanced over her shoulder, smiling back when he smiled. He seemed to approve of her outfit.

She wore a very short red dress with a paisley print on it, cut in a hillbilly design. Her hair was in two braids that fell over her full breasts, complete with red ribbon on the ends. She even had on black cowboy boots. The skirt was so short it made her long legs look amazing.

Jessica tried to ignore him, and knocked on Alex's door. "Your turn," she said as she entered the room. "But you better hurry. Gene looks hungry." Heat rushed through her cheeks.

. . .

*Alex

Alex didn't miss the look on Gene's face as he sauntered to his room. "Hungry like a wolf, maybe," she teased. "Maybe Tom and I should share the shower and save time."

"That's a great idea," Tom said, sticking his head in the room, and looking right over Jessica's head.

Jessica glanced over her shoulder. "You know, so far, you're the only guy that's truly made me feel short. You're a... A... Mountain."

Alex's eyes widened when Tom smiled. Her mind flashed back to her conversation with Jessica about the fortune teller. She had told her a mountain would change her life.

"Yeah, I've been called that before," he said. He let Jessica out of the room before he stepped in.

Alex was searching her closet for something to wear. Her mind was still racing over what the fortune teller had said and the words of the mysterious visitor.

"Love is a powerful thing, especially when true love is involved."

Could this really be happening? Dare she believe in something so far-fetched?

Tom broke her from her intense thoughts. "You all right?"

"I can't decide what to wear," she complained, trying to cover her ass. She wasn't ready to talk to him about her thoughts.

"Wear whatever you want." Tom shrugged.

"No, I can't! Jessica looks all cute with her pigtails. I can't be frumpy in jeans."

He crossed the room, reached over her head, and pulled out the first thing his hands touched. "Maybe this," he asked.

Alex looked the dress over he'd pulled out. It was a turquoise and gold brocade strapless dress. She smiled. She hadn't thought of that one, but it would leave her shoulders bare, and she hoped Tom would find them kissable tonight.

"Why don't you go have a quick shower while I grab my clothes?" Tom said.

Tom let himself into the bathroom before Alex had turned off the shower. He was shaving at the sink when she turned off the water and pulled back the curtain.

Her body flushed with warmth and embarrassment. For some reason, she felt shy being naked in front of him, despite all they'd done together. She quickly grabbed her towel and headed for the door.

"Alex, are you all right?" he asked, making eye contact through the reflection in the mirror.

"Yeah, I just didn't hear you come in," she said. "But the shower is all yours." She slipped out the door before he could say anything else.

Back in her room, she took a minute to center herself before she got dressed.

Why am I being so shy?

Tom had seen her naked before, and he'd had had no complaints. That was before.

She was still reeling from the fact that a preternatural stranger had literally touched her. Not to mention that the woman had said that Tom was her true love, but if he was, then how was she going to deal with him leaving?

Alex slipped on the dress Tom had chosen. It enhanced her waist and full breasts. It always made her feel sexy.

How did he know?

Tom knocked on her door a few minutes later. He was wearing dark gray jeans, a white T-shirt, and a blue flannel.

She'd just finished blow-drying her hair when she opened the door.

"You ready?" Tom asked.

"Yes." She smiled up at him.

. . .

Alex laughed when Tom handed her a second drink. She'd gotten shaky on the way to the bar, so he'd ordered her a drink the moment they walked in. Her shock at what had happened, all they'd been through, was finally sinking in.

Even when she'd worked in the forest service, she usually had one good cry in the shower after a big rescue or fire.

It was her body's way of dealing with the stress she'd suppressed during the emergency. This time, she didn't have the luxury of a long shower to cope, and her nerves were fraying.

Three drinks later, Tom still hadn't convinced her to eat yet, so the liquor was hitting her hard. She wasn't alone.

Jessica was rather tipsy as well.

Her bestie had plowed through her burger, proving to Gene she could eat a burger as big as his.

Then they started on drinks.

Gene said Jessica couldn't keep up with him. He was drinking beers, and she'd taken to the harder stuff. She was one drink behind him but argued that she was drinking more liquor by percentage.

Alex just smirked at their silly argument. Whether or not they agreed, Gene and Jessica were well-matched. Her best friend had met someone who could handle her.

The jukebox was playing a variety of tunes in the background. Jessica hadn't truly been listening, but Alex had been singing quietly along to the music.

As the song changed, Jessica stopped in the middle of her argument with Gene. She knew the song. She jumped up, grabbed Alex's hand, and dragged her to the space between the pool table and the dining area. *You Shook Me All Night'* started playing and they laughed as they began line dancing.

Gene

Gene and Tom both watched, in awe as the girls did some

thrusting moves, then swooped down low, rolling their backsides out as they came up.

He almost fell out of his chair when Jessica did a kick-ball-change, her foot kicking over her head.

She flashed him the black shorts worn under her little dress.

Alex and Jessica turned in unison, and he watched the back of the dance.

His cousin's eyes were also on the girls—specifically Alex.

Gene loved seeing Jessica run her hands over her beautiful backside just for him. He had to adjust his pants to be more comfortable, because damn, she sure could make his blood boil.

The song ended, and they came back to the table, full of laughter and out of breath.

The alcohol-fueled Jessica brought out a boldness he doubted she otherwise had.

She crawled onto his lap, wrapping one arm around his neck.

The server came back to see if anyone needed a refill.

Both girls put in an order.

"Is there any way I could convince you to come in and teach that dance to the bartender and other servers? I think it might help with tips," the server said.

"Um," Jessica began. "We just moved into town, so I'm sure we will be back in again. I would love to teach it."

The server smiled big, thanking her, and scurried off to get their drinks.

When her drink arrived, Jessica got off Gene's lap, stepped over to Alex, and held it up to toast.

Her friend looked at her funny. "We can't do the Jolly Roger toast. It wouldn't be right," Alex said.

Jessica grinned wickedly and leaned in close to her friend, "I've got it! What goes down in the Mustang, stays in the Mustang!"

Gene stuck his face in between the girls. "Unless it leaves a sticky mess, then you get to clean it out of the Mustang."

Jessica turned her head and captured his lips.

It took him by surprise but he didn't let it show. He snaked his fingers into her thick hair, where the braid started at the nape of her neck and he took control of the kiss.

Jessica slid her arms around his neck, bringing him in closer. Then she whispered against his lips, "I guess we better not leave a mess."

"Are you sure?" He'd never take advantage of a woman, drunk or not.

"Absolutely."

Gene turned to Alex, who was just as intoxicated as her friend. "Alex, should I trust her?"

"Absolutely," she slurred.

Gene grabbed Jessica's hand and started toward the door.

*Tom

Tom just rolled his eyes at his cousin. This was the guy he knew. Only thinking about what his body wanted, never his heart.

Typical Gene.

Alex stood in front of him, her posture and expression timid. "How are you feeling, Tom?"

He took her hand and pulled her closer. She stood in between his knees. "Like a new man. I saw you heal me. I heard what the stranger said." He'd waited to bring that up—he'd been waffling as to whether he should or not—but what they'd said in the caves was more important than he ever could've guessed.

Jade.

He knew better than to question when Fate was shared with them. He just didn't expect to actually *find* his soulmate.

But how could he tell her?

Would she think him crazy?

There was no doubt they had a connection. But could he say the word *love* and mean it?

Yes.

"I guess we're gonna have to talk about that," she whispered.

It had been a long day, and she had a lot to process. He wouldn't put that on her shoulders, yet. "Yeah. But not until tomorrow. Let's just be here, in the moment. And I'd like to dance with you." He stood and took her to the spot where she'd danced with Jessica.

It was awkward at first, trying to two-step to the slow song, since he was so tall, but they made it work.

Gene

Gene opened the passenger door to the Mustang, pushed the bucket seat forward and motioned for Jessica to get in.

She giggled after she'd climbed in and tried to slide across the leather bench but couldn't, and started laughing again.

"What's so funny?" he asked, trying to get in with little luck.

"My butt is stuck to the seat. I can't slide over." Sliding across leather with bare skin just didn't work.

"Then lift your ass up and get over."

"Wow. You're bossy," Jessica teased.

"And you're drunk."

She finally moved far enough that he could get in and shut the car door. "Nope. Not drunk. Just happily buzzed," she said. She looked around her surroundings, then back at Gene. "You know, the last time I was in the backseat of a car like this was with Alex."

Gene arched an eyebrow and smirked.

Jessica smacked him. "Not like that, you pervert. We were really drunk at a bar where we used to live. I don't remember why we were in the back," she slurred.

He slid his hand up her left thigh, bringing her attention back to him.

She leaned close, their lips just a breath apart. "I've never made out in the back of a car before," she whispered before letting him capture her lips.

"Oh, I think we'll be doing more than making out," Gene said quietly when they came up for air.

He pulled Jessica back to him, and she crawled onto his lap, straddling him the best she could in the car.

Gene ran his hands up and down the outside of her thighs and without thought, she rocked as she claimed his lips.

His pants were far too tight, and she wasn't helping.

Their kisses grew more demanding.

Gene left her soft skin to cup her full breasts through the material she wore. He wished they were both naked but would work with the situation. He slid his hands down her body, then he slipped his hand between them and undid his pants, freeing himself from the tight restraint.

Jessica

Jessica gasped when he pushed at her core with just her shorts and panties between them.

She'd never done something like this. It just wasn't her style. Yet she was burning for him, and the liquor didn't help.

Without moving off Gene, she reached down and pulled the crotch of her shorts and undies aside, just enough to allow herself to be impaled.

She rode him hard and fast, right there in the dark parking lot of the bar.

They fogged the windows up, and the only light came from the neon sign above the door of the bar.

It didn't matter.

Jessica was too wound up to care.

She wasn't conscious of being in a car until she rose a little too high and hit her head on the low roof. She laughed and leaned down to bury her face in the crook of Gene's neck, inhaling his smell.

He bucked slightly under her, causing her to move again, faster, harder.

Jessica threw her head back and cried out in pleasure as her body built with intense pressure, becoming a blissfully violent orgasm.

The tightening of her muscles did Gene in. Without warning, his body exploded, filling her with his hot release.

She collapsed forward on him, snuggling her face in Gene's shoulder. "I can't believe we just did that," she whispered.

"Neither can I," Gene said.

"Um," Jessica whispered. "I think we're gonna leave a mess in the car."

CHAPTER
TWENTY-FOUR

Tom

Tom held tight to Alex as they drifted to the music.

He rested his cheek on the top of her head. It felt so right.

As they spun around, Jessica and Gene still hadn't returned to the table.

Alex lifted her head to look up at Tom. "Where'd they go?"

Tom groaned.

"You don't think they—"

"Yes," he said.

Alex laughed.

Tom was glad she found the humor in it. It would've been a long walk back to the farm if she hadn't.

"How long should we give them?" she asked.

"Oh, I don't know... How about if we get a little food in you, then we'll worry about them."

"Fine. I know if I don't eat something soon, I'm gonna have a wicked hangover."

They each ordered a burger and were about halfway done when Jessica slipped into the ladies' room.

"Should you go check on her?" Tom asked.

"Nope!"

He lifted his head in surprise.

"If what we think happened, actually did, then it will just embarrass her if I call her on it."

"So, what should we do?" he asked.

"I recommend you get those keys 'cause I ain't riding to the farm in that back seat."

Tom laughed at the disgusted face she made.

Alex leaned forward in the front seat of the Mustang, as they drove toward the farm.

Gene and Jessica were snuggled in the back seat, whispering to each other in between kisses, while Tom did his best to ignore them.

Alex didn't seem to be paying them any attention, either.

"Whatcha looking at?" Tom asked.

"The moon. It's red." She glanced at him. "'A red moon rises.'"

Tom nodded. "'Blood has been spilled this night.'"

She smiled. "You do know the Lord of the Rings!"

"I told you I did."

They pulled back into the farm and parked.

Gene and Jessica headed inside, holding hands, but Alex stayed next to the Mustang.

Tom came around and leaned against the car next to her.

She was gazing up at the red moon.

"You all right?" he asked.

"Yeah, it was just a long and scary day." She sighed.

He watched her expression, hoping she'd relax after realizing the danger was over.

They'd destroyed the Wendigo, so she had nothing more to worry about.

However, Alex didn't relax.

As she gazed up at the moon, she began chewing her lip, as if she was trying to expect what was coming next.

"You seem troubled," Tom whispered. He wanted to touch her, pull her to him, but he waited for her to talk. Maybe she needed to work things out in her head.

"Sorry," she said, finally turning to face him. "Old habits die hard."

"What habit would that be?"

"Some cultures believe that a red moon is an ill omen," Alex said, "and it never seems to fail that something bad happens when there is a red moon."

Tom pulled her into his arms. He couldn't be separated from her any longer.

She stood between his legs, and crossed her wrists behind his head.

"I think we've had enough bad things happen for today. What's say we not borrow any more trouble?" He smiled down at her.

Alex ran her fingers up into his thick hair. "I don't know how you do it."

"What's that?" he asked.

"You've spent your whole life saving people from this stuff."

Tom shrugged. "It's what we do. I guess it's like the family business."

She chuckled. "You say it like it's your motto."

"I guess it is," he admitted, breaking eye contact and pulling her against him. He enjoyed the warmth of her embrace. However, he could feel her body tensing slightly. Instinct shouted that she'd ask what neither of them wanted to think about.

"You're leaving tomorrow, aren't you?" her voice wavered.

He let out a big breath. "I don't want to, but Gene will be itching for a new case."

"Well, I still have a ghost. That's a case, right?" Alex asked, in a soft, innocent voice.

Tom laughed, "Yes, you do, but I'm not sure you want to get rid of this ghost."

Alex looked up, disappointment written across her beautiful face.

He dipped down and kissed her softly. Her lips were plump and inviting. "Should we go up to bed?" he asked when she pulled away.

She nodded, with a shy edge that made him want her even more.

Tom took her hand, and kissed her knuckles before they headed into the house, fingers entwined.

Jessica

Jessica rolled over in bed. Her head pounded violently. She pressed a hand to her forehead until she was awake enough to realize she was going to have to take something to get rid of it.

She flipped off the covers, only to discover she was still in her dress from last night. Her cheeks flushed with a heated embarrassment.

Jessica remembered going to the tavern with Alex and the guys, trying to out-drink Gene, but he'd cheated and only drank beer while she was drinking mixed drinks. She recalled line-dancing beside Alex, then heading out to the car with Gene.

Crawling out of bed, she went into the bathroom. One looked in the mirror and had her appalled. She had lipstick smeared on her face, her eyes were coated in a dark circle of mascara, and eyeliner, and her braids had come loose.

She washed her face and brushed her teeth, then unbraided and brushed her hair. When she looked semi-decent, she changed and went downstairs to get some ibuprofen.

The house was still quiet, so she assumed Alex and Tom were still asleep.

She pushed open the kitchen door and surprise washed over her, because they were sitting at the kitchen table.

"Good morning, Jessica," Tom said, looking up from Alex.

Her bestie glanced her way. "Good morning."

Jessica groaned and went to the cupboard on the right. The door opened of its own accord, showing her the bottle of ibuprofin.

"Thanks, Grams," she said without thinking.

"That good huh?" Alex teased.

"My head's killing me."

"I bet," Tom said. "I'm surprised you're standing, after all those shots last night."

Jessica frowned and glanced at the tall guy. She didn't remember doing any shots. Although, it would explain her headache.

"Tom! That's not nice!" Alex said, smacking his hand. "Jessica, you weren't doing shots, but you had a lot to drink."

Tom smirked. "I'm pretty sure you drank Gene under the table, though."

"Who did?" Gene said, pushing through door open.

"Jessica did," Alex said with a wink, and a smart-ass smile.

Gene smiled at her as if she were a piece of meat. "That's my kinda woman." He wrapped his arms around her waist.

Jessica was torn between pride and offense. She may have drunk him under the table, but that wasn't what she was normally like.

She tried to always be ladylike with proper etiquette. Maybe Gene only wanted the dark side of her personality, which rarely made an appearance. However, she couldn't be mad at him. Not after what they'd shared—including killing the Wendigo.

Jessica looked up into his intense green eyes and smiled. She fit so perfectly next to him.

Gene let her go and headed to the coffee pot, grabbing two cups from the drying rack. He filled them both, handing her the first cup.

Jessica didn't miss that he left room for sugar and cream. Had he remembered from the day before, or just assumed she wanted cream added? She smiled again, as she took the mug. Either way, getting her coffee was sweet.

Gene leaned into the counter, crossing one bare foot over the other, putting all his weight against the old wood. It creaked a protest, so he stood back up, as if embarrassed. "So, did anyone else catch what the crazy lady said yesterday?"

Jessica felt her heart thunder in rapid succession. Was he really bringing up the 'love' stuff? "I, uh…" she stammered.

"She said she heard you through her kin. Think one of the victims was related to her?" Gene continued.

Jessica wasn't sure if she was relieved or saddened that *that* was what he got out of her words. "She didn't look like any of them."

"That's the thing with Fayefolk, though. They can make themselves look like anyone. It's called glamouring. So she might look completely different at any given time. I mean, she had the same colored eyes as you, Jessica. That's one of the reasons they are so hard to find. There's not a lot of information on Fayefolk that isn't bullshit, children's stories, kind of stuff."

"So how do we find out who her kin was, so we can thank them?" Alex asked.

"It's unlikely we will ever find out," Tom chimed in. "I'm just grateful she did."

"I think we all are," Jessica said.

Gene shifted, reaching to get more coffee. "So, what's the plan for today?" he asked, completely changing the subject.

Tom and Alex looked at each other.

Jessica couldn't stop smiling. What he'd said meant Gene wasn't rushing his cousin out the door and onto another case.

Her heart skipped. He'd stay a bit longer.

She stepped up to him, also still barefoot, and kissed his cheek. Without her heels on, she had to push to her toes, and it made her heart race. "I know what we could do," she whispered, not too quietly in his ear.

Tom laughed from across the room.

"You should clean the back seat of the Mustang before you do anything," Alex said, smirking.

Jessica looked at her friend, arching an eyebrow, then she glanced at Gene.

He had a huge grin on his face.

Her heart was in her throat. She'd thought they'd cleaned up after themselves last night, and that her friend had no clue of their sexcapade.

"Let's go sit down," Gene said, taking her hand and leading her out of the kitchen. He kept going, taking them outside and to the front steps.

Jessica's tummy swirled, and radiated discomfort.

Was that it?

Had I gotten sick in the car and can't remember?

Gene wouldn't be smiling if that had happened.

Her hand went to her stomach automatically.

He suggested they sit and offered her a hand to help her down. He sat beside her, taking a sip of his coffee, as if he needed to take his time.

Jessica frowned and irritation jumped up from her cycloning stomach as the silence dragged on. "Dammit, Gene! What am I missing?"

He laughed, which only made her more upset.

She punched his arm, which she instantly regretted, because her knuckles throbbed.

His biceps were rock-hard.

She shook her hand, trying to take the sting out.

Gene took her hand and kissed her knuckles.

Not the reaction she'd expected.

"What you did was give me one of the most amazing nights of my life," he whispered.

Jessica frowned.

"You don't remember us going out to the car?"

She nodded.

"We did something I've fantasized about, but never actually done. And my little lady has a naughty side. That's just so... so...hot."

Her cheeks rushed with heat, and her tummy warmed again, but this time it wasn't irritated. "I remember that. I still can't believe I was that brazen. But, why are Alex and Tom talking about cleaning the Mustang? I thought we took care of things last night."

Gene lifted her chin so she'd have to meet his eyes. He leaned in to gently kiss her. "We did. But it was pretty easy for them to guess where we ran off to and what we got up to." He stood and offered her his hand. "I made a promise, and I think it's time I upheld it."

Jessica took his offered hand, not standing up yet, just looking up at him.

He smiled, and the lines around his beautiful green eyes appeared.

They made her melt.

She stood and let him lead her into the house, ignoring Alex and Tom, going up the stairs, and straight to her room.

Gene shut the door quietly, not saying a word.

Jessica just stood there a moment. What should she do? Hadn't she just suggested that they should have sex when they were in the kitchen? Now she couldn't move; felt shy.

He stepped closer, cupping her cheeks, his fingers wrapping around the nape of her neck. Without a word, he took possession of her lips, taking her breath away with a sweet, yet intense kiss.

Their tongues did a dance as his hands slid down her neck, over her shoulder, and halfway down her bare arms, which were now wrapped around him. He reached for the side zipper of her dress, but got it stuck at the waistband.

Jessica had to finish undoing it for him.

Gene grabbed the short hem and pulled the dress over her

head, smiling at the red lace bra that held her full breasts in place. He dropped the dress to the floor and dipped down to kiss the creamy swell of her right breast.

She moaned.

He straightened to kiss her soft lips. Then pulled back ever so slightly to whisper to her. "This is a first for me, and I've been waiting to do this. Soft and slow…"

His words sent shivers over her skin as he stepped her closer to the bed.

Jessica reached for the hem of his shirt and pulled it over his head, dropping it by her dress. She ran her hands over his smooth muscled chest. She was so lucky, even if he was only hers for a short time.

They reached the bed, and she sat down slowly; the bed creaking softly.

Gene shucked his jeans.

He wasn't trying to be seductive, but Jessica couldn't take her eyes off him as he moved close to her.

Gene gently urged her back. Without saying a word, he slipped off her panties.

He kept his promise.

Jessica had never been so thoroughly, quietly, and intensely made love to. As they lay in her bed, her head on his damp chest, she ran little swirls around and around. She brought her fingers up to his tattoo and traced the star.

The star he wore over his heart.

"Gene," she whispered. "What does your tattoo stand for?"

He was quiet for a minute, shooting worry up from her gut.

"It's a protection symbol, a *Unicursal Hexagram*. It symbolizes the sun and moon ruling over the four elements. It's also known as the *Guardian Spirit*. The tribal flames represent the continuous pattern of life and death, the path of the moon and sun. Basically, it protects us."

"From what?" she asked.

"Well, anything that tries to take over our bodies, suppressing our spirit. Tom and I have had them for a few years now. A demon briefly possessed Tom, so we got them tattooed on to prevent that from ever happening again."

Jessica cocked her head to one side. "Would it still work if it was a necklace?"

"Yeah. That's actually what we started with. A family friend gave them to us, but we made it permanent. We may still have them somewhere in the Mustang."

"Gene, speaking of the Mustang, I've never done anything like that before," she whispered to him.

Gene chuckled.

Jessica met his green eyes.

"Yeah, it was a little different." He did not elaborate.

"You've never…?" she prompted.

He shook his head. "You rode me hard in the backseat without taking a stitch of clothing off. Don't take this wrong, but I've been with my fair share of naughty girls. But they were nothing compared to you."

Jessica blinked. Should she be insulted or flattered?

They'd just finished the most amazing sex she ever had in her entire life and he was talking about being with other girls!

She frowned and hurt assaulted.

Jessica wanted to push away, but Gene grabbed her shoulders.

"Oh, honey, it's not like that! Let me finish what I was trying to explain."

Now they were both sitting up, and Jessica was about ready to bolt from the bed.

"My point was, I've had naughty, which has always been my girl of choice. But you, you're something else. Jessica, you're a lady and you're sophisticated, yet you've got a sexy naughty side. You can kick ass as well as make a pie and likely could fix my car as well as I can. And those aren't even the important things about you. You're everything that I never knew I wanted."

She blinked again, as emotions hit her chest, spread out and made her eyes water.

His handsome face was so sincere, and it melted her heart.

Jessica moved back into his arms, hiding her face against his neck. She couldn't look at him, because her eyes burned with tears.

*Gene

What he'd said processed in his brain seconds after he'd said it. Gene needed to go.

Now.

He cleared his throat, trying to swallow the knot there, and excused himself, wrapping the sheet around his waist as he took off to the bathroom.

Gene didn't want to hurt her, it was the very last thing he wanted to do. But he couldn't stay in her bed—in her arms—and face his…feelings.

He started the water in the shower and needed a moment to himself to fix things.

How did I get myself into this situation?

He thought he'd fallen in love once before, and quickly learned that family life wasn't for him. He'd have to constantly put the ones he loved in danger, and it was hard enough having Tom in danger.

Gene knew what he needed to do. He reached to shut the water off when Jessica gently pulled the curtain open to step in.

It caught him off guard and he grabbed Jessica, ready to attack.

It only took him a heartbeat to realize, but his heart was racing, nonetheless.

He apologized, excused himself, and jumped out of the tub, leaving Jessica in obvious shock to shower alone.

CHAPTER
TWENTY-FIVE

Tom stood in the library, waiting for Alex to bring him a dusting rag.

They went through some books to see if they could find any more information to help with their ghost problem.

He pulled a leather-bound book from the shelf and thumbed through it. It was an old family photo album. Most of the pictures were black and white.

Tom smiled at several pictures of children posing in front of the house. Three children, two girls, and a boy. As he turned the pages, the girls were grown up, but no sign of the boy. Then pictures of new people and new babies appeared. A modern-day photo showed a couple holding a dark-haired baby that very well could be Jessica.

He stopped on a page, his breathing paused briefly as he looked at the picture.

"This should get us started," Alex said.

Tom jumped at her voice. His attention had been on the book fully, and he hadn't heard her approach.

"What is it?" She closed the distance to him, strips of cloths in both hands.

"Jessica said the ghost called her Edith, right?"

"Yeah."

He lowered the book so Alex could see what he was looking at.

She gasped.

There was a black-and-white picture of two young women in clothes likely from the 1920s, standing in front of the farmhouse. Someone had carefully written two names under the photo. Barbara and Edith. The woman on the right had caught their attention.

It was Jessica.

"How is that possible?" Alex asked, a frown marring her pretty face.

"It says Edith." Tom flipped back to the front page, where a family tree had been written out. The handwriting changed with each new branch.

They found the name Edith and followed it.

Edith was the first daughter born to Judith and George Fergeson. She had a younger sister, Barabra. Barbara married Otto Pike and had a son, who died at the age of fifteen. Edith had married John Witte and had two daughters, Marjory and Beatrice. Marjory had never married. Beatrice had married Alan Marr and had one daughter, Jenifer. Jessica's mother.

"So Edith was Jessica's great-grandmother?" Alex asked.

"According to this family tree. But Jessica is the spitting image. Odd. But that makes sense as to why the ghost of Great-Great-Grandma is protective. She thinks Jessica is her daughter."

"Tom!" Gene yelled, bursting into the living room, his duffle bag slung over his shoulder. "We gotta get the hell out of here. Go get your bag."

He reared back, glanced at his cousin's disappearing form, then back at Alex.

Her eyes filled with tears, but he didn't pause to comfort his love.

He rushed outside after his cousin. "Gene!" Tom called out as he took the steps two at a time. "What the hell?"

Gene was sitting in the passenger seat of the Mustang, with his legs outside the car as he dug in the glove box. He had something dangling from his hand and he pushed to his feet. "Where is your stuff?"

Tom frowned. "Did you get a call?"

He closed the distance to him, pushing the items into Tom's chest. "Yeah, a call. We gotta go. *Now*. Give these to Alex and get your shit. We're leaving." Gene went back to the driver's side of his car. "Now, Tom!"

Confusion slowed his step, despite his cousin's urgency. Tom looked at what Gene had given him.

It was the protection amulets their uncle had given them so many years before. Tom hadn't known Gene had held onto them.

Evidently, his cousin wanted him to give them to Jessica and Alex.

"Tom?" Her call was hesitant.

He opened the screen door and pulled her small body against his much larger form. Tom rested his cheek on the top of her head for a moment, just holding her.

Tom didn't want to let go. He'd just dreamt that night that they stayed on the farm and he and Alex had started a family and were raising horses.

Whoever had called Gene must've had something urgent for him to be in such a rush to leave.

Tom kissed the top of Alex's head. "We have to go, Alex."

"I know." Her voice broke as she stepped back.

Gene revved the engine.

Tom reluctantly stepped back. He slipped one of the amulets

over her head to let it rest on her breasts. He handed the other one to her. "Please give this to Jessica and always wear them. Never take them off. They'll protect you from anything trying to possess you."

Alex tried to say something, but Gene honked the horn.

Tom turned and headed up the stairs to collect his things.

*Alex

Alex stood as he thundered up the stairs. Why wasn't Jessica there to say goodbye to Gene?

The horn blared again.

Maybe they'd already said goodbye, and it hadn't gone well.

When Tom came back down, it would be hard to let him go, but it had to be done. He was leaving to save another life. Alex needed to be proud of him, but it was hard not to be selfish and want him to stay.

Tom rushed to her, pulled her close, and kissed her with such passion, that the kiss told her without the words that he didn't want to leave.

"What about our ghost, Tom? You can't leave yet." She couldn't let go of him.

"She's not going to hurt you. I think she's trying to protect her family. Keep the salt if you're worried. I'll come back as soon as I can to figure out what you girls want us to do about her. Her spirit should be set free. I wish I had time. But I'll be back."

"Tom?" Alex cried one last time as he let her go and hurried out the door.

"I'll call you," he called over his shoulder while he rushed to the car and his impatient cousin.

. . .

Alex sat on the couch, her face in her hands as she cried. She couldn't understand how she had fallen so hard, so fast. She wiped her eyes, but more tears came.

She should check on Jessica. They would need each other to cope with the boys leaving.

However, Alex heard something she didn't expect from the vicinity of her best friend's room. The door was open.

Jessica was singing happily to herself, dancing around her room.

Alex moved inside, just in time to see Jessica spin around as she made the bed.

She had such a big smile on her face that quickly disappeared when she saw Alex's tear-streaked face.

"Alex! What's wrong?" Her bestie stopped dead in her tracks.

There was no way Gene had told her he and Tom were leaving.

She must not know.

"They're gone," was all Alex could manage.

Jessica

Jessica didn't understand what her friend had said.

Then Alex's words hit her, and she ran to look out the window.

Sure enough, the Mustang was gone.

Jessica ran past Alex to the room Gene had been in. His duffle was gone. There was nothing of his in the room.

She slowly went to Alex's room, too afraid of what she would find. Sure enough, Tom's things were gone, too.

Her knees were weak, and she leaned against the doorjamb to hold herself up. It didn't help; Jessica slipped to the floor. She looked up as Alex stood over her. "He didn't say goodbye," was all Jessica could say as her tears fell.

Alex sat beside her on the floor and hugged her tight.

Usually, Jessica was the strong one that held Alex together. She couldn't do it right now. She clung to her best friend.

"I'm sure they'll be back after they go help whoever called. Gene looked like it was truly urgent. Someone must really be in danger," Alex said, trying to get Jessica up off the floor.

"I thought he was happy. He said I was everything he never knew he wanted," she said, as she wiped at her tears.

"Tom said he'd call. When he does, we'll find out when they're coming back. We have a ghost to help, after all."

Alex dug in her dress pocket. She pulled something out and handed it to Jessica. "Gene said to give this to you. Tom said we should never take them off."

She took it, turning it over in her hand.

Gene must care about her, just a little, to leave it with her. When he'd said his uncle gave it to them, there was something in his voice that said the person was gone. It likely meant a lot to him.

He gave it to her.

Jessica slipped it over her head. The metal felt warm against her bare skin. She held the amulet close. It might be the only reminder Gene was real, in case he never came back.

EPILOGUE

*Tom

Gene sped down the dirt road away from the farm, and Tom pulled the beat-up Atlas out of the glove box.

He quickly thumbed through to find the quickest route to get to Esbon, Kansas, where their temporary home was—inside an old, abandoned train depot. It was small, but it was theirs. The first Gene'd had since he was a small child. It wasn't much, but it was home.

"Gene? Did you realize when we hop on Highway 183, it's a straight shot to the depot? We're less than two and a half hours away from the girls." His voice was more chipper than he had intended to, but it just made him feel comfortable knowing that he could get to Alex quickly if need be.

It wouldn't take him days, just a few hours.

Gene grunted, nodding. He didn't really reply, just popped in a cassette that was on the top of the shoebox of music on the dashboard, and turned the music up loud.

It was *Asia*.

Not one of Gene's favorites, but he didn't seem to care. His cousin sang along to a few songs.

It wasn't often Gene sang along, and usually, he was being funny about it. This time, he was *actually* singing all the lyrics.

When the fourth song began, Gene was no longer singing. Tom stopped and listened to the words as it was apparent his cousin was wrapped up in them.

The song spoke of a man out of money, out of luck, and broken inside. He was praying for a miracle. He'd been abused, misused, and unloved. Until he'd met her. He sang that he'd do whatever it takes to get her back. He's asking for her forgiveness.

Tom narrowed his eyes and watched his cousin's face.

He hadn't seen pain like that in a long time.

He took a deep breath and turned down the music. "Gene, there was no phone call, was there?" Tom tried to keep his voice calm, but he missed Alex already.

"Yeah, it's Fillie. She needs us back at the depot. Right now. It's life or death." His cousin's voice wasn't very convincing.

"Dude. She's in Florida. What's this really about?" He frowned, trying to keep his temper in check.

Gene let out a deep sigh, like he'd been holding his breath for the past hour. "I can't do it, Tom," he whispered.

"Can't do what?" Tom barked. He'd left Alex when everything in him screamed he should have stayed. His cousin pulled him away. "I thought you liked her. Does Jessica even know we left?"

His cousin gripped the steering wheel until the leather creaked a protest. "I walked away. I had to. *We* had to," Gene said it with resolve, like those words explained it all.

"What the hell is that supposed to mean?"

He didn't answer.

A few minutes went by before the silence was too much for Tom. "Dammit, Gene! I just don't get you! You had the girl of your dreams right in front of you. And you just left! Dragging me away from the first real slice of happiness I've had since... since..."

Gene pulled the Mustang off the side of the road and slammed on the brakes. He killed the engine and climbed out of the car, slamming the door behind him.

Tom got out, too, so angry all he could see was red.

His cousin ran his hands over his face, as if he was trying to hide, but not fast enough.

There was no missing the tears.

Gene leaned against the hood of the car, Tom still standing by the passenger door.

He said nothing, just watched his cousin take a shaky breath before he spoke. "I love her! Is that what you want to hear? I love her, Tom. And that's gonna get her killed if I stay."

Tom sighed, and walked around the car, going to Gene.

"I'm sure she hates me, because yeah, I left without a word. But it's for the better. Everyone I love dies. And I can't bury any more friends." He wiped at his face again.

"Gene, there was a better way to handle this. Didn't you think I'd want a say in our future? Maybe I wanted to stay. We've stopped the apocalypse, more than once, and pulled each other back from hell in one form or another. And lost too many friends to count. So maybe it's time we got our happy ending. Why not pass the mantle to another hunter and put away our guns?" Tom could hear the plea in his own ears, and damn, his whole body wanted it—wanted Alex.

"You know we don't get happy endings," Gene bit out.

"Why not?" Tom pushed. "We deserve it."

His cousin huffed. "That's not the point, Tom. We don't get happy endings because we bring them. If we weren't hunters, other people would be burying their friends and family. We do our job so others can live. We had to leave. So, Jessica and Alex can live. We did our job, and it's time to move on. Time to find someone else to save." He pushed off the hood and went to the driver's door. "Let's move, dude. I have a feeling something big is waiting at the depot."

Tom sighed. Right now was not the time to change Gene's mind.

One way or another, he'd find the road back to Alex, the woman he loved; his soulmate.

ABOUT THE AUTHOR

Andrea Hurtt is an emerging author of various romance categories. She enjoys writing a little bit of everything.

Andrea has been a dental assistant, a stay at home mom, owned her own clothing store, was a clothing designer with a vintage-inspired clothing line, Amaryllis Designs, even won Omaha Fashion Week for Top Designer in her category, and Top Boutique for Cancer Survivor Night.

During covid she wrote four novel, an award winning TV pilot screenplay, and moved to Vancouver, BC to pursue acting.

Andrea currently spends her days either writing books or making #EmotionalSupportPillows and traveling around the USA with the cast and fans of the CW TV show Supernatural.

She is the mother or two children, a cat and a dog, and is a proud Army wife; residing in a haunted Victorian mansion the MidWest.

ABOUT THE AUTHOR

This is Linda Stecker's first published novel. She enjoys horseback riding, knitting and traveling.
A chance encounter at a community theater audition she didn't even want to attend, Linda and Andrea became quick friends after being thrown on stage together. She has been writing with Andrea Hurtt ever since.

ALSO BY ANDREA HURTT

<u>**Razor's Edge Rockstar Series**</u>

Masquerade - Book One

Undone - Prequel

Unmistakable - Book Two

Incomplete - Book Three

<u>**Love Under Lockdown Series/ Short Stories**</u>

Acting The Part

Truth or Dare

<u>**Demons Within Us Series**</u>

Nebraska Nights

COMING SOON

<u>**Razor's Edge Rockstar Romance Series**</u>

Drowning - Book Four

Inconsolable - Book Five

AVAILABLE ON AMAZON AND ANDREAHURTT.COM